DEDICATION

I would like to dedicate this book and say
to thank you to my Earth Angel David
and his friends, who inspire and motivate
me to achieve things that I never dreamt,
were possible.

INTRODUCTION

Legally I cannot use Lyrics or Music because of Copyright but I can use song titles so a total of 1616 song titles (Italicized) have been used to make this story possible. Also due to the nature of my books; legally I must place a Reference,.(exactly the way they are down loaded) and Bibliography in the back of the book.

Follow the story of Mrs. Jones and Miss. Jones and how gossip can make a rumour of the unknown truth become something completely different as it is being spread and how it can hurt and change the lives of the ones at the centre of the gossip.

Who was the one with the blue eyes who helped Miss Jones get home and also helped her son to get someone to love him?

Discover the new friends they make, who don't believe the rumors but learn and accept the truth about the Joneses.

ACKNOWLEDGEMENTS

I would like to thank my daughters, Jenny and Kylie for their positive but critical input in the first draft of this book and all the help and support that they have given me throughout the Song Title Series books. With taking their input to mind, I have improved the book.

I would also like to thank my son Peter and his family for their support and help in keeping me grounded.

I would like to thank Kay and Julie for their patience and understanding whilst teaching me and giving me the skills to present my unique books in the best way possible.

I would also like to thank everyone else who has helped me bring this book to life and to you for purchasing it.

THE UNKNOWN FACTS

It was the *end of May,* and the weather was unusual for that time of the year because it was *a foggy day* and not a clear bright sunny day in their part of Delaware but that didn't stop *Emily* and *Danny Boy* from going for a walk down the *Boulevard of Broken Dreams* to the *Broadway* to have morning coffee at the *Ca C'est L'Amour* Cafe.

Just like every morning, they were meeting *sweet Georgia Brown* and Harry there.

Danny Boy thought "I *don't get around much anymore* since the accident almost two months ago that took my best friend Joanna and left me with a badly dislocated hip, a broken leg and some internal injuries.

The driver of the big green car had a *cold, cold heart* because they didn't even stop to see if we were alright.

I laid there helplessly because of my injuries but I could see that Joanna was badly injured and she was *drifting* in and out of consciousness; even though she seemed to be more concerned about me.

I told her "*Hold on* and *don't worry 'bout me at this moment;* just concentrate on yourself and don't move, help will be here at any minute now. Just lay there and go *dream dancing* amongst the *autumn leaves* in the park like we did last year when it was *autumn in New York* and here.

Joanna never made it and was *buried in blue;* her favourite blue coat the following day.

It was two years ago that Emily and I had moved here from San Francisco due to some family issues, but *I left my heart in San Francisco* because I had left all my good friends there. We moved to the country for a while and I liked it there because *it's so peaceful in the country* and *for once in my life* I felt like I could be *young and foolish* again.

We were living *the good life* in a rented cottage on an estate, until that *white Christmas* when the *poor little rich girl* from the big house got a *fever* after being caught out in the *stormy weather.*

She was rushed to the *Chicago* Children's Hospital and was a very sick little girl for a few months but she told her parents "I am getting better and *I'll be home for Christmas* so that I can sing the family *Christmas song* with you on Christmas Eve."

She did go home for Christmas but that *poor little rich girl* couldn't live in the country anymore because she had to be nearer to the medical facilities. So the family had to sell the entire estate and moved to *Hollywood* and joined all *the folks that live on the hill* and that's when we moved here.

Ah! Here comes *sweet Georgia Brown* and Harry. I don't really know if I am looking forward to *a conversation with Harry* because it can be *a blessing and a curse.* After a moment with me, he'll keep saying "*Have I told you lately.*" when he knows that he hasn't.

I wonder why he is dressed in that silly looking *top hat, white tie and tails* at this hour of the morning. Oh well, I suppose he'll tell me soon enough.

Sweet Georgia Brown ordered *tea for two* and Harry *come by me* on my left side and sat down almost hitting my bad leg.

I said to him "*Jeepers creepers* Harry, *how insensitive* can you be, you almost got me on my bad leg and what's with the get up; *I've never seen* you dressed like that before. *I remember you* telling me quite a few times that you would never wear anything like that, because you only like the *bare necessities.*"

Harry replied "Yeah, I know I did, but 'cos you *don't get around much anymore,* then you don't know that there is this agent hanging around town and he is looking for someone to star opposite Miss *Solitaire* in her next commercial for *The Valentino Tango* Biscuit Company."

"Wow." I said "if you get the part, what would the pay be? *There'll be some changes made* to your life, so doesn't that bother you?"

Harry said "I haven't got the part yet, but if I did, the pay is cash each month and a year's supply of *The Valentino Tango* Beef Jerky Biscuits and *The Valentino Tango* Rawhide Bag.

You know that I might even be able to finally approach that beautiful, sexy Miss Jones. I love watching her walk by with that *blue velvet* ribbon tied in her hair.

All of me will do *what ever it takes* for her to notice me, even if it means me getting dressed up in this gear every day.

Would you get dressed up everyday to get someone to notice you?"

"Nah, *give me the simple life*. I'm one of those who won't worry in the slightest if you take me as I am or leave me alone. So *have you met Miss Jones* yet?" I asked.

Harry looked down and said "Well, not really. We haven't formally been introduced; but when I pass her on the street, I have *the brightest smile in town* for *the most beautiful girl in the world.*"

I said "I don't know if you knew, but *when Joanna loved me* she told me that she used to run around with Miss Jones in her younger years. The park that they used to hang around in was the one near *the pawnbroker on Green Dolphin Street."*

Harry asked "*Have you met Miss Jones?"*

"Have I met Miss Jones? Yep, I have, before she went from *rags to riches*. She acts like a *sophisticated lady* but *the lady is a tramp* still. I don't know if it was just *girl talk* but I heard that she used to meet up with *Hudson Bommer,* when he was *just a boy* down on *the Boulevard of Broken Dreams*.

There's a small hotel where the girls went when they had *love for sale*. They called it The *Blue Light Red Light* Hotel because you could get the *blues in the night* from the red hot *love for sale* from the females there." I replied.

"You must be kidding me! Don't tell me that *the girl I love* went from *rags to riches* by having her *love for sale*. If it's true, then *the lady is a tramp* but then again you said that it could have been just *girl talk*.

As time goes by, situations change and now she may feel that because of her past and the gossip, she is caught *between the devil and the deep blue sea."* said Harry.

I said to him "If you want to find out if it's true, go ask a few of the older lads who have grown up around here and knew her when she was younger. Just say *"Have you met Miss Jones?"* and then listen to what they have to say. You'll find that *everybody's talkin'* about her these days.

Hey look, here comes *Anema E Core.* I don't know why he was given that name 'cos he's known only as *E.* He used to live next door to Miss Jones so he should be able to tell you a bit about her."

Harry called E over, and asked him *"Have you met Miss Jones?"*

"Unfortunately I have." said E *"Have you met Miss Jones?* By the look on your face, I would say not. *I could write a book* about her.

I had to spend a few weeks over at her place while the rest of the family spent *April in Paris*. I had an ear infection at the time so I wasn't allowed to fly and my family couldn't change their plans and wait for me to get better. I would have loved to have spent *April in Paris*.

Now, Miss Jones, she used to share her *candy kisses* treats with me and she would say "One for me and *one for my baby.*"

She was such a good looking *baby* that she became so *easy to love*. She liked to play games all the time; *night and day* and the only way to stop her so you could get some rest was to say "*Alright, Okay, you win.*"

Well, *I fall in love too easily* and that's what I did with her. That *crazy little thing called love* use to hood wink me quickly, back in those days. Mind you, her *crazy love* and her *anything goes* attitude was *all my tomorrows,* or so I thought.

Then one day I said to her "*All I do is dream of you* and you can *fly me to the moon* at anytime.

For once in my life, I wanna be around the girl I love, the most beautiful girl in the world, forever for now or until someone changes the stars and moon.

Well, *someone turned the moon upside down* a week later, *something* went wrong in her family and her father moved to *Chicago* and the rest of the family moved into a *caravan* down by *Chelsea Bridge* for awhile before moving into a house on the *Boulevard of Broken Dreams.*

I went back home to my family and I didn't get to see her very often after that.

The family used to come over every now and then and I told her on her last visit "My heart beats for you in a strong way that *ev'ry time we say goodbye* and *after you've gone; so beats my heart for you* that much, that I find that it isn't long after that, that *here comes that heartache again."*

Then one day the family came over without her and I never saw her again.

I heard that she started sneaking out and running wild around the *Muskrat*

Ramble Pool Hall where *Mac the Knife* hung out. At the time *Mac the Knife* was the King of broken hearts because he would steal your girl from you, leaving you broken hearted.

Sometimes *I wish I were in love again, like* I was with her, but for that to happen; well, *it's like reaching for the moon*. That was in the time of the *beautiful madness* of my youth and now that I'm older, I think that *I'm the king of broken hearts*.

I'm just a lucky so and so that I didn't stay with her and now, just *being alive,* well, *it's alright with me. If I love again, the second time around* will be different.

Guys I have to be going now but if you happen to run into Miss Jones, just say that we've talked and *just say I love her still.*"

"Thanks for stopping and talking to us E. Have a good day." I said.

"Gee." said Harry "I didn't know that he used to live next door to Miss Jones. I think that at the time, he was living on the *street of dreams*.

You heard him say quite openly "*I fall in love too easily.*" so who else has he been in love with, and it ending with a *heartache* tonight.

Taking a chance on love in *this funny world* means that you have to be willing to *take the "A" train clear out of this world* for that special someone."

"*When Joanna loved me,* I knew that *I've never been in love before* so I was *lost in the stars* for awhile. *Time after time,* Joanna would tell me that *I'm always chasing rainbows* and I should get them out of my system before she would *come fly with me* to the *blue moon* and *have a good time.*

When Joanna joined our family, she was a little older than me, she really was a *stranger in paradise,* my paradise and I thought that there's *something in your smile* that is in the ingredients in the *recipe for love.*

She had a few *sleepless* nights to begin with, but somewhere along the way she became *daddy's little girl* and that melted her *cold, cold heart.*

We became *just friends* until one day when we were out walking, she saw *Stella by starlight,* her old flat mate, with *Coco* her boyfriend making out, in broad daylight, in the parking lot of the *Bayou Maharajah* Indian Restaurant.

Joanna approached her and said "*Stella by starlight, it had to be you,* didn't it. I see that it didn't take you long to start *steppin' out with my baby* after I left the apartment block.

Oh, don't move, just *stay where you are,* and watch me as *I'm walkin'* away from the pair of you with my head held high."

And then she said to Coco "*There'll be no teardrops tonight* and *I won't cry anymore* for you and what we had because I see that *it don't mean a thing* to you. *This can't be love* that you have for me."

As she walked away with me, she looked back at the couple and said "Enjoy the food here at the *Bayou Maharaja;* if you're lucky it may not upset your stomachs too much."

That night *the gentle rain* and the soft *summer wind* brought that *stranger in paradise* closer to me. I had seen a different side of Joanna that day and I thought to myself "She is strong and dignified. I'll have to *straighten up and fly right* if *I want to ride the glory train* with her and I'll do *whatever it takes* to do it because *I wanna be around* her for the rest of my life. *There'll be some changes made* around here and the first one will have to be with me."

"How did you straighten yourself up?" asked Harry.

I told him "The neighbours on the other side were *Antonia* and *Buena Sera* who met down in *Besame Muncho* when the family went on holidays there and they moved up here six months before I moved in next door to them. They had a son called *Bisco* who eventually moved in with someone else down on the *Boulevard of Broken Hearts*.

He told his parents that "*I've grown accustomed to her face* but *I've come home again* to give you some news."

In his *Bisco mushroom version* voice he said "We are moving to *Edelweiss,* you know, the *city of angels,* in a couple of weeks. *Because of you,* mother, I have learnt *what is this thing called love* is all about and father; you have taught me the *rules of the road* and life which I won't forget.

I will try to bring her by before we leave. *Wait to you see her,* then you will know why I love her. *My heart stood still* when I saw her and *my heart tells me* that she is the one for me. *We are in love* and I know there will be a lot of responsibilities put on us if we *marry young* and start a family."

Antonia asked his son "*What are you afraid of?* I can see it in your eyes and I hear a little of it in your voice".

Bisco said "I'm afraid that if we have any troubles, *who can I turn to* for help or advice? You'll be too far away for me to contact at a *moment's notice* because you don't have the phone on here."

His mother said *in a mellow tone* "*The very thought of you* moving so far away upsets me a little but if you can't *stay where you are* then it's *just one of those things* that I will have to get used to.

Remember what we have taught you especially about being honest. *One lie leads to another* and then it will be *congratulations to someone* else that she will be able to trust.

Because of our nationality; we always *marry young* and we always *let there be love* both *night and day*. I know that *the best is yet to come* for you, so go, and *have a good time* with your new wife but did I hear you say "*Who can I turn to?*" when you need guidance or advice; why the angels of course.

You are going to live in the city of angels and they will be watching you; in fact, they are all over *this funny world* and they will help you. I did hear that an earth angel David helped my mother once in her hour of need."

Then his father said to him "You may not be able to bring her by before you go as the family could be too busy packing. I wish you all the best and please be careful travelling on *the long and winding road* near *O Sole Mio. This is all I ask.*"

I stopped talking for a moment and as I looked around I spotted an old friend and called to her "*Madonna, Madonna.* Hey, *Madonna, Madonna* come over here for a moment please."

Harry said "But how did you straighten yourself out?"

I said "I'll tell you later. Madonna went to school with Miss Jones. Get her to tell you about her experiences with Miss Jones."

OLD TRICKS, NEW TRICKS

Madonna walked gracefully over to the boys who were sitting down at the end of the table that was outside the café and said "Please don't get up. Danny, I heard about the accident and your terrible injuries and Joanna will be missed around these parts. How are you going?"

She looked at Harry and said "Hello, you must be new to town because I *haven't met you yet.* My name is Madonna."

Harry replied "No, I'm not new to town; I just don't get down this way much. Danny was saying that you used to go to school with Miss Jones. What was she like?"

The look in Madonna's eyes really told the story "*Have you met Miss Jones* yet? Don't answer that, by the look on your face, she hasn't met you yet.

Where do I begin? As a young thing, she was very elegant at the beginning but with the trouble in the family, and the moving, she became like all the others down her end of the *Boulevard of Broken Dreams*.

I think living in the *caravan* park had something to do with it as well because someone with a *cold, cold heart* who also lived in the park gave her some *end credit roll* and that made her catch that *crazy little thing called love*.

Yes, *someone turned the moon upside down* and put *stardust* in her eyes, but no-one knows who the *candy man* was.

No one will ever know who used to feed her the *candy kisses* that sent her *out of this world*.

Who ever it was, told her that she would go from *rags to riches,* living in *Hollywood* but he would have to go there and talk with the agents and they would need a down payment to find her a leading role in a movie.

He took all she had and took off, telling her "Not to *do nothin' till you hear from me* or till I come and get you."

She never heard from him again. She was still growing up and I think that the *growing pains* she had were mainly from *falling in love with love* and anyone who spoke to her in a tender voice and promised her the world.

I ran into her one day and she was a mess so we walked down to the park, the one down by *the pawnbroker on Green Dolphin Street* and we had a long chat.

For once in my life, I felt sorry for her and *all of me* wanted to help her sort her life out. She said that she would do *whatever it takes* to get her life back on track, so I got her into the *New York State Of Mind* Institute but she ran away from there because she said "*My teacher is a zombie.*"

She heard that the *Paramount Fanfare* was looking for females to star in the *Lullaby Of Broadway* Vaudeville Show.

She actually got a small part in it and travelled down on the *Atchison, Topeka and the Santa Fe* railroad towards Washington, but some of the cast were dropped from the show in a small town called *Tangerine* and she was one of them.

The *Lullaby Of Broadway* only lasted until *maybe September*. Then in October, some of the cast auditioned for the *Mountain Greenery* Circus, unfortunately for Miss Jones, she wasn't hired because she couldn't do many *tricks* as she was mainly a dancer not an acrobat and they were looking for acts that could *move the crowded* Big Top.

Paramount Fanfare began auditioning for another Vaudeville act called the *Tin Roof Blues* and this time she got the part of the *little clown* who began *dancing in the dark* once someone said "*Music Maestro, please.*"

It was her *time to smile* as the show travelled to the *Mardi Gras in New Orleans* but one day in the tent she slipped because it was *too darn hot* and she badly pulled a muscle in her back and couldn't continue dancing.

Doctor Jazz examined her but after two weeks; she still couldn't do her full dancing routine so they replaced her. She left the show and made it back to *Manhattan*.

In *Manhattan,* she heard this *crazy rhythm* and went to investigate where it was coming from. The *crazy rhythm* was coming from the *Samba De Orfeu* Club and while she was listening to the music and watching the others dancing, she was approached by *Samba Do Aviao* himself.

He told her that he liked her moves; however, with a little bit of training, she would make a great *little dancing girl.* There would be a small fee if she wanted to learn the moves from him and if she became good enough, he would give her some work dancing in the *Samba De Orfeu* Club.

She said "*I've got five dollars,* will that be enough?"

Samba smiled and only took three dollars and she began training that very day. She tried very hard to get the moves right, but she just couldn't get the rhythm right in her head that corresponded with the moves.

Samba said to her "*Listen little girl, make it easy on yourself.*

Dancing is one of *my favorite things* in life, so don't try to do it. Where do you feel that *crazy rhythm* the most?"

She replied "I feel it *here in my heart* the most and *at this moment* my whole *body and soul* just wants to move by itself."

"Good, good." Samba replied "now let's do a little *experiment. Close your eyes* and *with imagination,* let's pretend that *I only have eyes for you* and that I *haven't met you yet.* We *got the gate on the Golden Gate* Bridge between us and you want me to come through it.

Listen little girl; listen to the rhythm, feel it, this one is just a *little waltz* music; move slow and smooth like you are dancing *cheek to cheek* with me. Yes that's right.

Now, we are going to do the same *experiment* with *Joe Avery's piece* that has a little of that *crazy rhythm* in it. This music is a bit quicker but it is still as smooth and it's a dance where you have to *change partners,* so you won't be dancing *cheek to cheek* with me or anyone else.

Your new partner will dance differently to me so you will have to learn to adjust your moves to his very quickly. Yes, I think that you have the moves and rhythm adjusted correctly.

Now, that dance has ended and they are now playing music that has a lot of that *crazy rhythm* in it. In this *experiment,* we are *in San Francisco* and again we *got the gate on the Golden Gate* Bridge between us, *close your eyes* and *with imagination,* I want you to bring me through that gate to dance with you, but you have to do it with your dance moves. That's perfect.

Now let's begin this first routine with plenty of *sway* of the body. No, no, I said *sway.* You were doing it before, now you're dancing like a *paper doll."*

She told him that she couldn't do it and said "*Let's call the whole thing off.* Maybe it's *just one of those things* because *it only happens when I dance with you."*

Samba approached her and said *tenderly "Baby don't you quit now.* When you have to dance at any time; especially in front of others, just *close your eyes* and *with imagination,* take me onto the dance floor and give me some *crazy love* from your moves and you can get *lost in the stars* with me.

If you *hear me in the harmony,* then you can hear that *crazy rhythm* or any other music in the back ground but you won't be concentrating on it. You might even feel a sort of *disco sensation* going on that will seem like *it's magic.* Now *let's face the music and dance* again and *let's begin* with the *sway,* not a movement that looks like a wave.

Oh, yes, that is so beautiful to watch. You are so *young and warm and wonderful* and *you're easy to dance with* and because you seem so natural with your moves, I'm going to put you on a contract right now.

You can have a *lazy afternoon* tomorrow and you can start at the club tomorrow night.

Be at the club around night fall and see *Mam'selle* and she will fit you with the necessary costume items."

Manhattan was a *sleepless* city where a lot of males of all ages and nationalities went from *rags to riches* very quickly and *taking a chance on love* with different females was *something* that was second nature to them.

They would often say to the female they were with at the time "*You go to my head* so *come fly with me. With plenty of money and you,* we can live *the good life* and *while the music plays on,* we can go *dancing in the dark* every night.

You must have been a beautiful baby because *the shadow of your smile* and *the way you look tonight* tells me that *there will never be another you* for me and *you'll never find another love like mine.*

You'll never get away from me and you won't want to because you will never have the *blues in the night* so come on, *taking a chance on love* with me will mean that you will be changing your life from *rags to riches."*

She arrived at the club early and Mam'selle looked at her and said "We have a *Broadway* talent scout coming in tonight looking for dancers to star in the revival of *Lullaby Of Broadway* Vaudeville show, so *the way you look tonight* will be very important. Yes, you will look beautiful with this *blue velvet* scarf around your neck.

Because you are *young and warm and wonderful,* I think that you can do the *moondance* to the *theme "Valley Of The Dolls"* and *Mood Indigo* will join you for your next dance to *the trolley song* that really has that *crazy rhythm*.

Now remember what Samba has taught you and if you want a spot in the *Lullaby Of Broadway,* you will have to do *whatever it takes* to impress the talent scout."

It was show time and she remembered what Samba had told her "*Close your eyes* and *with imagination take me* out onto the dance floor and give me some *crazy love* with your *crazy rhythm.*"

The Trolley Song routine was an instant hit with the crowd.

After her performance was over, she was called over to the table where the talent scout sat and as she approached, she heard a male say "One for me and *one for my baby.*" and it was there that she was given a drink by someone with a *cold, cold heart* because the *love scene,* as she soon found out, was more than just a kiss.

She realized that all the females working in the club had their *love for sale* to the male clientele.

She saw Samba and went up to him and cried, "This is an establishment for females with *love for sale* and mine isn't. I don't believe that I should have to put mine up for sale to someone I don't know and don't love."

This time Samba didn't talk *tenderly* when he said "*Don't cry baby.* You signed a contract and *you belong to me, forever for now.*

You are now in *Manhattan* working, not with the *Mountain Greenery* Circus down at the *Mardi Gras in New Orleans*.

Having your *love for sale* is what you will have to have to go from *rags to riches* and to living *the good life*.

There's no business like show business and because of you, I have had a good night with the patrons. They all love *the way you look tonight* and they all want to see you dance some more so I think that you should get back up on that stage and dance to the slower *Army Air Corps Song* and don't forget that wonderful *sway*."

When the next dance set was finished, Samba went up to her and said angrily "*Where did the magic go* from your routine. You looked like the last big *wave* that hit *way down yonder in New Orleans*. Come with me *my pretty shoo-gah, I've got a great idea. Put on a happy face* because *when you're smiling* from the inside, it shows through your whole *body and soul*.

I am going to introduce you to a couple

of our special, regular clients, who *haven't met you yet*.

Until yesterday they were living on *the Boulevard Of Broken Dreams* down in the Broncs. They worked *day in, day out* on a *tug boat* but they didn't give up and they finally went from *rags to riches* when they found a diamond mine *in the middle of an island* off the coast of South America whilst on their holidays."

The *intro* to the special clients, Armond, Tex and Sandy, was made and she thought "*If I only had a brain* that thought quicker, then I should have realized that Samba was just *a weaver of dreams*. He gave *the good life* a sweet look by feeding me *a spoonful of sugar* and saying that "*You'll never know* what *a taste of honey* is like when it's coming from *a sleepin' bee*."

She told me that there was *something in Sandy's eyes* and his *smile* that she could *surrender* to and they told her that he was different to all the other males in the club.

Sandy and Miss Jones danced the *Moondance* and they talked. He said to her "Please *save the last dance for me*. I have to leave for about an hour but I'll be back, I promise. Please *do nothin' till you hear from me* later tonight."

He left the club but he was back an hour later with a female companion.

Before the last dance began, Sandy ordered three drinks saying "There's one for me, one for Miss Jones and *one for my baby*."

The last dance began to play so we got up and danced. During the dance, Sandy said "The female with me is from *Our Lady Of Fatima* School Of Dance and I think that she maybe able to help you. *The shadow of your smile* tells me that in the *beautiful madness* of Samba's words and the *crazy rhythm* of his music, you had a *day dream* of becoming a big star.

The song is ended so we have to stop dancing, but now, do exactly as I say.

Go to Samba and say "*I was lost, I was drifting* and I was a *lonely girl*, a *stranger in paradise,* your paradise and *you took advantage of me* and *my reverie* to make something of myself.

Because of you I am caught *between the devil and the deep blue sea* but you *can't buy me love* and my love will no longer be for sale. I will dance for you but *that's all.*

My contract with you only states that I will dance for you and nowhere in it does it say that I have *love for sale.*

I won't cry anymore over doing something that isn't right for me." and then I want you to go, get your things and leave, but try not to let anyone see you leave. Don't stop and talk to anyone and don't linger or you'll be sorry. *There's a small hotel* two doors down and we will meet you outside there."

The *Our Lady Of Fatima* School Of Dance was just a front for another organization that rescued young females from clubs and from the streets who didn't want to have their *love for sale.*

She met Sandy outside the hotel in *a little street where old friends meet* and he, with the help of the other female, whose *vocation* was, to help her to come *all the way* back home where she belonged.

Sandy told her that *the best is yet to come* and *the moment of truth* was coming because her family had reported her missing to the authorities. Sandy and the other female helped her from being locked up by hiding her, before being returned home and she said that she was so glad that her family wanted to "*take me back again.*"

But living on *the Boulevard of Broken Dreams* had its set backs because nine weeks later, she gave birth to a baby boy, whom she called Sandy.

Miss Jones thought "*Jeepers creepers, I've never seen* such a beautiful *baby* before. *I will live my life* for you because *you're nobody till somebody loves you* and that somebody will be me."

The family was not impressed about the new arrival and had Sandy adopted out about a month later.

The look *in Sandy's eyes* as he left his mother was confusing but his mother said to him "*Don't cry baby. I can't give you anything but love* and *at this moment* I think that it's best that you go with this other family so I can sort myself out.

I know that there will be *heartache tonight* for both of us but *the best is yet to come* for you and you will realize this when you are older.

You will be living with a family *who cares* about you and you know that I'm not well and have to have an operation that will not allow me to have anymore babies or even care for you properly."

Sandy said "*I wanna be around* to take care of you but *I'll go* if you say I have to, but I don't like *the very thought of you* being here all on your own; especially because you're not well. *There will never be another you* for me even though my new adopted mother will give me a good home and love but *who can I turn to* if I need some advice and you're not there?

I know that I'm just a *baby* now and I know that I will have *growing pains* for a few years but what about you, how will you manage without me?"

His mother said "*Don't worry 'bout me, I'll be fine.* I have heard from others who have been troubled that they turned to the angels for help or advice. I was told, just to ask for whatever, advice, help or need, at the present time for what is bothering you and just *watch what happens* as what you ask for, you may get. It may not be in the way that you are expecting it to happen, but it will happen.

When I was younger, I got into a situation that I thought I couldn't get out of but *I wished on the moon* and asked the angels for help and they did help me to get back home.

Now *put on a happy face* and give me a big *smile* and *promise me you'll remember* to *try a little tenderness* with the young ones who may get a bit rough at times."

That night as Sandy lay on his bed he thought, "*Here comes that heartache again* and I think *I'm the king of broken hearts* but *how can you mend a broken heart?*

I will do as mom said and I will talk to the angels and ask them to send me *someone to love* and while I wait to see what happens, *I won't cry anymore.*"

The following morning, Sandy was woken by the warm gentle touch of small hands picking him up. He opened his eyes to see a pair of *angel eyes* staring back at him and the feel of a kiss on his nose. A *love scene* without *love letters* between him and the female holding him could have been written right there and then.

Sandy thought "*I see your face before me* and it was not the one I saw yesterday and *for once in my life,* my very short life, *here in my heart* I feel that *taking a chance on love* with you would be the best thing for me.

I *haven't met you yet,* well, not really, so let's *just say I love her* already. *Because of you* I now feel that my *life is beautiful* and I won't have any *heartache tonight* before I sleep.

Mom was right in how the angels give to us what we ask for in *this funny world*. *I'm glad there is you* little one, *just kiss me* again and *you could make me smile again* especially in my heart and *you can depend on me* to make you *smile* whenever you are feeling down."

Miss Jones told me that she had the operation and she now wakes up everyday with "*Good morning heartache*."

For some reason, when the family goes out, they leave her at home and she wonders "Why don't they *take me* with them like they used to do?"

Any way, one day the family went out and they forgot to shut the door properly behind them, so she thought that she would follow them discreetly to see where they were going.

While following the family; she ran into a male who she had met briefly from San Francisco, and he instantly recognized her and wanted to meet with her; but when she told him that she didn't do that anymore he said to her "Once a female has *love for sale*, she always has her *love for sale*. My good buddy *Mack The Knife* would certainly be interested in knowing about you."

Her reply to him was "*It had to be you* that I ran into, didn't it? *Then was then and now is now. I don't get around much anymore* because I spend *my time of day* with my family and I don't *stay awake when lights are low* with *reflections* of the past.

For once in my life, I don't have to worry about any *heartache tonight* or say "*Here comes that heartache again." I let a song go out of my heart* the day I left *Manhattan."*

Madonna heard the Library clock strike eight o'clock and said "I must fly; *I didn't know what time it was.* I'll be late for my hair appointment at the *My Blue Heaven* Salon."

"*Jeepers creepers."* said Harry "if *that's entertainment* and what it can do to you then *I'll guess I'll have to change my plans."*

"Now *hold on."* I said "you're not like her and you're auditioning for something quite different, besides you're a male and you don't live down that end of *the Boulevard of Broken Dreams*. I doubt that Miss *Solitaire* is anything like Miss Jones.

Working in advertising would be *nice work if you can get it* and it's different from working on the stage, like in the *Lullaby Of Broadway.*"

"Yeah, I guess you're right. Advertising can be done *all in fun* and is not as serious as in other types of acting. Now are you going to tell me how you straighten yourself out?"

INGREDIENTS FOR LOVE

"Antonia told me how to straighten myself out and when you think about it, it's really so easy because it is just plain common sense." I said to Harry.

Antonia said "*I could write a book* about this topic. *What the world needs now is love,* but many folks keep asking the same old question; *what is this thing called love* and when you find out what it is, how do you help it grow so that your *love is here to stay* in your heart forever; no matter what life throws at you?

There are different kinds of love for different situations. A mother's love for her *baby* is different from her love for her husband, and both of those kinds of love are different from the love she has for her neighbour.

When I was a young one back in *Besame Mucho,* I was often told a local legend by the oldies and I will tell you now.

Once upon a time, there was a *cinnamon sinner,* who was actually a *voodoo child,* who lived under one of the many *bridges* by a *lazy* river in a neighbouring town and he used to enjoy *quiet nights of quiet stars*.

Many folks who crossed over the *bridges* used to make fun of him and they all laughed at him.

Yes, he was a *lazybones* when it came to actually working but he was very good in using *that old black magic* to get what he wanted.

He could change the weather just by saying *let it snow! let it snow! let it snow!* and sure enough, it would start snowing even in the middle of spring or summer.

The folks passing over the bridge would say, "*Spring is here* and look it's snowing. I've never seen a *winter wonderland* at the *end of May*. With the way our weather has been lately, *it might as well be spring* when we are supposed to be having a *white Christmas* or we could end up with an *Indian summer* in the middle of autumn with the *autumn leaves* scattered on the ground."

One day he saw this beautiful young female walking over the bridge wearing a *blue velvet* ribbon in her hair and he realized that he lived on the *lonely side* of life. Even thought he had seen this female many times, he hadn't really noticed her and every day after that, he used to wait for her to pass by.

One *lazy afternoon*, he waited for her, with a big bunch of *roses of yesterday,* to cross the bridge so that he could speak to her. She did *smile* and accept the *roses of yesterday* but she didn't stay and talk with him.

Everyday for a week he gave her a bunch of *roses of yesterday,* and everyday she would *smile* and take the bunch of *roses of yesterday* but she still wouldn't speak to him.

On the following day as he handed her the bunch of *roses of yesterday,* he blocked her path hoping that *maybe this time* she would talk to him and he asked her why she wouldn't stay and speak with him."

She said to him "I live in *Rocket City* Drive near the *Bayou Maharajah* Park, amongst *the folks who live on the hill* and you live here in *solitude* under these bridges by this *lazy river.*

Do you know what it means to this *poor little rich girl* if she is seen talking to you?

My folks have asked me everyday from whom I have been getting the roses and I have told them from a *stranger in Paradise* Valley. *One lie leads to another* and now they want to come and meet the *stranger in Paradise* Valley.

When I get home, I'll have to tell my folks that the *stranger in Paradise* Valley has moved on, and even though they *haven't met you yet,* what do you think they would say or do if they knew that it was you who gave me the roses?

You and I could never have any kind of relationship unless you moved out from under the bridges and move into one of the houses up on *Bourbon Street Parade.*

Now, please don't approach me again, *this is all I ask.*"

And she continued walking on without giving him a chance to say anything more.

That night, he lay under the bridge as *the gentle rain* was falling and he thought "*How come you do me like you do. I can't help falling in love* with you and *I can't give you anything but love* and *candy kisses* but *I wanna be loved* by you because you are so *easy to love.*

Every night, *all I do is dream of you* and tonight *I'll dream of you again.* Why does this *crazy little thing call love* have me *bewitched?"*

That *old devil moon* finally came out that night and the *cinnamon sinner* thought, "I can usually get what I want by using *that old black magic,* and so in the *lazy afternoon* of tomorrow *when lights are low,* I will use some magic on her as she walks by.

I'll take her to *Chicago* or to *Oompa Loompa* town that is *east of the sun and west of the moon. There's a small hotel* there where we can stay at *night and day* and *no one will ever know* that *it's magic* that keeps her with me."

The following *lazy afternoon,* he lay in wait for his *la vie en rose* to cross over the bridge where he would give *one last pitch* for her to spend time with him and if that didn't work, then he would use his magic on her, but she didn't come.

As he waited for her the next day he heard some other folks who were crossing the bridge talking about a couple of young females who had caught a *fever* after being caught in *the gentle rain*. So he thought that she must have been one of them because she hadn't crossed over the bridge for the past two days.

The next couple of nights, the *old devil moon* was shining as a *blue moon* and he would *dream* that he was with *the most beautiful girl in the world, not as a stranger* but as her *lover*. The *love scene* that played in his head always ended up with her *gone with the wind* and with him waking up saying *here comes that heart ache again*.

He thought to himself "*I'm the king of broken hearts* and it seems that trying to get you to talk with me; well, *it's like reaching for the moon,* the *blue moon* that shines amongst *so many stars.*"

He hadn't seen his female for over a week and he became worried about her. Had her *fever* been worse than what he had heard or was she just avoiding him and he made the decision that he would try and find her the following day.

That night he tried to settle down to get some sleep but because of his *heartache tonight,* he just couldn't get into a comfortable position or chase her face from his mind.

It was during the night that a stranger came up to him and asked "Mind if I spend a few hours here by this *lazy river* to rest? I've come a long way and I'm pretty tired and I want to calm down *the beat of my heart* a bit before I continue my journey."

Cinnamon said "No, I don't mind. Who are you and where you from, stranger. I know that you're not from around these parts because you look different from the folks that live around here.

You have amazing blue eyes and you make me feel so calm. No one has ever made me feel like this before. Are you using magic on me?"

The stranger said "No, I'm not using magic on you; I don't have to, besides it's wrong to use magic on someone, especially if it is for all the wrong reasons.

I am known as the *Midnight Rabbit* and I come from the *merry old land of Oz;* Australia.

I hopped aboard a plane six weeks ago and landed in San Francisco, where I have just spent three weeks with a sweet little playboy bunny, I think that *I left my heart in San Francisco* with her but I know that *I fall in love too easily* so I'm glad to be back on the road again. It's the *s'wonderful memories,* that's all I have of her and *they can't take that away from me.*

At this moment, I wish I were in love *again* because *how can you mend a broken heart* and stop that *heartache tonight* from coming back?

You can't; it's *just one of those things* that life throws at you so you can learn and grow stronger from them.

Some folks work very hard for *the good life,* but for others, they're born into it and they find it very hard to see others for who they are.

Some folks *haven't met you yet* so they don't know you, just like me sitting here with you now; *you don't know me,* yet you seem to be comfortable around me.

All around *this funny world,* every thing, whether, human, animal, bird, fish or plant is different; even identical twins are different and you don't know how you are going to be accepted and *only you* can take the first step to find out.

The young female that has captured your heart, has been very ill with the *fever* but she has missed seeing you because *everybody has the blues* every now and then and you are able to cheer her up and chase those blues away for a while.

Her family's story of going from *rags to riches* was made possible through a *golden ticket*. Yes, that's right, a *golden ticket*.

Two years ago she was living in a *caravan* that was a *nowhere with love* in it and she picked up the ticket from the side of the road. She took the ticket *home* and gave it to her mother who had already bought a ticket and was listening to the radio for the winning numbers. The ticket that she had found had all the winning numbers on it.

The announcer said "*Congratulations to someone* out there as we know there is a winner."

The mother looked down at her and patted her on the head and said "*Have I told you lately* that you are a very good girl and now you are my special girl and *I'm glad there is you* in my life. We can now afford to move out of this caravan and live a comfortable life in town."

I could write a book on how and what others would do and do, do and have done to go from *rags to riches* and to get what they think is the good life. I have asked many of them and they have told me *these foolish things* that they try.

Quite a few people have told me "*I wished on the moon.*" or they write a *grown up Christmas list* every year hoping that Santa may bring them something that will get them where they want to be.

The *funny thing* is; some never do find the good life even after they have gone from *rags to riches* because it can be *a blessing and a curse.*

Well, that may be good for others, *but not for me, give me the simple life* so that *anywhere I wander,* I will be happy. *As time goes by,* I will go back home and settle down but now my plans are for *anything goes* for *all my tomorrows.*

Before I go, I'll tell you another story.

Once there lived a fool who thought that he didn't need anybody except his pet and one day he said to his pet "*With plenty of money and you,* we can live *on the sunny side of the street forever for now;*"however, he was never happy and he used to wake up with that *here's that rainy day* feeling again *here in my heart. It don't mean a thing* if you have all you want and no one to share it with.

I wanna be loved and *I wanna be around* people who love me, even if it means that I *don't get around much anymore* like I can now. I may *cry me a river* at this time but one day someone will *come by me* and will *fly me to the moon.*

For once in my life, I've got the world on a string anywhere I wander and *somewhere along the way;* I am hoping that *some kind of wonderful* happening will *come by me* and bring me that special someone to whom I can say "*Life is beautiful. Life is a song* so *let's face the music and dance,* while we *keep smiling at trouble* and we'll also *keep the faith, baby.*"

You ask yourself "*Who can I turn to* when I have an issue to sort out?" and the answer is the angels. They really are there and they will help you if you ask them because they will help to *light the way* for you to get out of your darkness. Don't forget to thank the angels for their help, when you start getting out of your darkness and found your way.

The *recipe for love* is easy to remember; always be honest with yourself and others, treat others with respect and respect yourself, look into a mirror or window everyday and say to the *reflections* you see "*I see your face before me* so *whoever you are; I love you.*"because if you can love yourself, then you can love others.

Accept others for who they are and the most important thing is; you have to keep reminding yourself "*I've gotta be me* 'cos that's who I am and I can't be anything else."

I heard a noise and turned briefly to see what it was and when I turned back, the rabbit was gone but I did hear him say "*Supercalifragilisticexpialidocious.* I have *Georgia on my mind* so I'm going to hop over there even though *I left my heart in San Francisco.* God bless and peace be with you."

Cinnamon thought "Am I a *silly dreamer* or am I going crazy; a talking rabbit and *didn't he ramble on.*"

But as he lay there, the stuff that the rabbit had said to him started running through his head and some of it began to make sense.

He fell into a deep peaceful sleep and that morning, once it was light, he got himself ready and went over to see the female from the bridge.

It took him awhile to find her house near *Bayou Maharajah* Park and when he did, he was invited in by her mother and now they are *just friends* and visit each other often."

Antonia said "I believe the story that was told to me because *as time goes by,* you see and hear about different things that others go through and know that *there'll be some changes made* to sort that out.

Time after time, you see who has learnt by their past mistakes and who hasn't.

Now, don't get me wrong, in their *beautiful madness,* everybody makes mistakes but owning up to them and being willing to change so that in *the second time around* if the issue arises, you are unlikely to make the mistake again.

If I could give you more advice; it would only be to remind you to always be yourself. *Let yourself go* and be crazy when it's time to be crazy but be serious when it's time to be serious and others will get to know and love the real you.

It is very hard to be someone you're not, because the real you will sneak out when you least expect it and others will notice that you are not being you and you are not being honest with yourself. If people don't like you for that, then just say to yourself "*It's alright with me.*" because not everybody likes everyone else. Now have I confused you?"

I replied "No, not really but it does give me something to think about. I know that in *moments like this,* it is hard to absorb all the information immediately and I know that *it's easy for you to say* because it helped you with your issue and the *way that I feel now;* I think that most of what you told me, will help me. Thank you it has been good talking with you."

"I'm confused." said Harry "What does all that mean and how did it straighten you out?"

"Well." I said "*You didn't know me when Joanna loved me.* There's me; *I'm always chasing rainbows* and *playin' with my friends* and there she was; *the most beautiful girl in the world,* just sitting and watching the world go by from *out of the window* of our favourite room."

"But how did Antonia's story change you?" Harry said impatiently.

"If you *hold on* a bit, I'll tell you." I said "I lay on my bed that night and thought about what I had been told and what I needed to do to win Joanna over. I guess *I'll have to change my plans* and stay home more and *anywhere I wander* with the guys, I'll have to make sure that I don't *fall in love too easily.*

Once upon a time when I was with the guys, it would be *anything goes* and sometimes we would sneak out to go *dancing in the dark.* We would say to any female that we met "*Tender is the night* with the *old devil moon* shining down on us so *let's face the music and dance while the music plays on.*"

One night a few of us were walking down *a little street where old friends meet,* when something made me stop and hide with the guys in some bushes near by.

We all heard, as *a nightingale sang in Berkley Square,* the sound of the authority's vehicle and their voices; they were looking for us. *All of me* just wanted to get out of there, but if any of us moved, we all would have been caught. Then *a nightingale sang in Berkley Square* again and the authority drove away.

One of the guys said "Did you hear, as *a nightingale sang in Berkley Square,* that the authority were going to raid the dance later on tonight and take anyone that was there into custody. Some of our closest friends will be *stompin' at the*

Savoy and will be in serious trouble tonight."

"Not if I can help it." I said "I know a short cut through these bushes and if I run fast enough, I might be able to just beat them and warn the others to get out of there. *All of you* go home where you'll be safe."

The other guys said that they were going to come with me, so we took off and arrived at the dance *just in time* to warn the others.

Someone yelled out "*Look, look, look* here comes the authorities, get out and away as quick as you can. Go, go, go; get away from here."

When I got back home, Joanna saw that I was a bit shaken and asked me what was wrong so I told her the full story and then I said "While I was hiding in the bushes, *I thought about you* and I asked myself "What am I doing?"

For once in my life, I realized that *stompin' at the Savoy* was not how I wanted to spend the rest of my life. I would prefer to be *steppin' out with my baby* instead. *Because of you,* I was able to help my friends but I *ain't misbehavin'* ever again. I would prefer *taking a chance on love* with you if you would let me."

Then Joanna said "Tonight, I won't have to hide my face when I *cry me a river* as my *heartache tonight* won't be coming but *I can't give you anything but love*. For a long while, I have had the *blues in the night* and sometimes I had a *sleepless* night over you.

I used to be color blind when it came to love and now *I wish I was in love again* because *I left my heart in San Francisco* with my other family; then you came along.

I wanna be loved by you and *I wanna be around* you *night and day* because *you're all the world to me*. For me, *there will never be another you* and *you will never find another love like mine. I've got you under my skin* and *you'll never get away from me* and you won't want to leave."

I looked at her and said "*I can't believe that you're in love with me* and you never let it show.

How insensitive have I been? *All of me* was hoping that it was *never too late* to be loved by you. *Once there lived a fool on the street where you live* but now that fool has gone because my baby just cares for me and *my heart tells me* to never let you go. For me, *it had to be you* and no one else that I would give my love to."

Joanna said "*It had to be you* who wanted to change your life; I couldn't make you do it no matter how hard I tried. *The very thought* of you out with the boys dancing with other females used to make me jealous.

Oh, *I still get jealous* when we're out, but now, I know that *my baby just cares for me* so I won't have to worry about that anymore and I know that I won't be *kissing a fool* when I *kiss you*."

I looked at her and said "*Tender is the night* tonight so come here and *put your head on my shoulder* and *close your eyes*.

You won't be having any more *sleepless* nights over me from now on, so *good night my love, pleasant dreams."*

Alfie, Sonny and *Firefly* used to *come by me* every so often and try to get me to go out with them but I stayed home with Joanna instead.

I heard that one night the authorities finally caught them and they spent time in *St James Infirmary Blues* Reform School and *Sonny cried* every night he was there. After they were released, Alfie was still the same, he would still say *"Let the good times roll* and *let's face the music and dance."* as he went running around.

He got caught again, and for *the second time around,* his punishment was to spend a fortnight with someone *back on death* row and the rest of his time at the *Our Lady Of Fatima* Reform School for hardened runaways learning the *rules of the road* and life from old Count Basie.

Count Basie never had a *cold, cold heart* but he still used to always say *"Sing you sinners."* but *old Count Basie is gone* now and I've heard that the new teacher has a *cold, cold heart* and is harsher in his teaching style, but he still says "*Sing you sinners,* repent for your misdoings. Come on and *sing you sinners.*"

Harry said "I'm glad that you straightened yourself out and stayed with Joanna. I've heard that once you have been in *Our Lady Of Fatima*, your days are numbered so you *don't get around much anymore.*

You are really confined to home but if you get caught out on the streets again, you're a goner. *Because of you* and with all that I've heard so far, *for once in my life* I am glad to be *by myself.*"

Sweet Lorraine walked over to Emily and *sweet Georgia Brown* and said as she sat down "I saw you out here and I thought that I'd bring my coffee out here and join you for a bit. I also thought that I'd bring the guys out a drink as well.

Another one of my friends was passing and stopped for a quick chat.

THE HUMAN SIDE

Sweet Lorraine gave the boys their drinks and sat down with the other girls at the other end of the table. Emily and Georgia continued their conversation and included *sweet Lorraine* into it. Their conversation ended up being a three way one about Mrs. Jones, who until recently had lived *on the Boulevard Of Broken Dreams*.

Lorraine: "Wasn't Mrs. Jones lucky winning that holiday to Canada and coming home with that great looking guy who is an international pilot and flies around *this funny world* of ours all the time."

Georgia: "Yes, she was. The talk on the street is that he lives in a big, luxury estate on a hill in *Manhattan* and that *on a clear day* you can see right across the bay and the *summer wind* blows gently around the big house.

He has asked her to move in with him."

Lorraine: "I ran into her when I was with my mother in San Francisco last month; I was there visiting my parents and mom and I decided to go to do some shopping and mom knew her from when they were in summer camp together.

Me and Mrs. Jones met and had lunch at the *Azure* Country Club and she was telling me about her holiday and meeting her new boyfriend and how he had asked to her "Come and *fly with me* to Amsterdam tomorrow." but she said that unfortunately she couldn't go at such short notice."

Emily: "If that was me, I would be off with him like a bullet out of a gun. For once in my life, I wish that I could be as lucky as she was, in getting that pilot. I wonder if he has any single mates who look just like him."

Georgia: "Don't forget, she has that troublesome dog to attend to.

Remember when the dog got out the last time. She was gone for nearly a month and came home pregnant and Mrs. Jones had to give the pup away after it was born.

Mrs. Jones told me that she was thinking of giving the mother away as well but she said "I'll miss her because *I've grown accustomed to her face* and she is my only family now."

Emily: "And how was your holiday with your parents? Are they well and enjoying *the good life?*"

Lorraine: "My parents are very well. They have become members of the *Ca C'est L'Amour* Club and they go there quite frequently.

They have a friend named Sam, who seems to attract these two particular women to him and wherever *he is, they are* there beside him.

Sam has a girlfriend and he keeps telling these two women "*I love Samantha.*" but this hasn't stopped them from following him around."

Georgia: "Do you mean that anywhere that *he is, they are* there too? I bet that that would upset his girlfriend 'cos I know that if I was *steppin' out with my baby* for the evening, it would annoy me knowing they were hovering nearby. I would soon give those girls the *blues in the night* once I have told them to get lost."

Emily: "Okay; so you're saying that anywhere *he is, they are.*

So if he goes to the men's room, do they follow him in there as well and if the men's room has two doors, why doesn't he slip out the other door and leave them to stand there all *evenin'* waiting for him. I bet they would soon get the message."

They all laughed.

Lorraine: "I always enjoy my visits with my parents but when I get back here I feel as if *I left my heart in San Francisco* with them. I would move back there with them but *at this moment* of time, my job will come first and *while the music plays on*, I'll keep getting paid to play it.

The *Lullaby Of Broadway* musical has another four months to play in *Chicago* and then we go onto *Hollywood* for six months and then to San Francisco for six months."

Emily: "If you have that much work,

then what are you doing back here?"

Lorraine: "*I've come home again* because some of the band members were contracted to play on four floats in the *Bourbon Street Parade* this coming Saturday.

Nancy, Jill, Judy and *Avalon* are playing *Ravel, string quartet in F major* on the second to last float with Miss Classical Music, a couple of the girls are playing the *Russian Lullaby* on one float with a few members of the Russian Youth Orchestra and two floats behind them, two guys are playing with the *Basin Street Blues* band and because *I love a piano,* I get to play with the *Jazz Me Blues* band on the second float with Miss New Orleans.

Do you know what it means to Miss New Orleans to be the

second float in this *Bourbon Street Parade?"*

Georgia: *"It had to be you* to get the best position; anyway, why is this particular parade so important, that entries come from all over the world? *It amazes me* on how you manage to get the best jobs going.

All of my life, I have given the *best of me* to what I'm doing *day in, day out* especially at work, but when it comes to the conclusion *Lester leaps in just in time* to take the honours. *The last payday* of every month, the person who gets the most honours gets a bonus and he is always getting it.

Why does it have to be me who keeps coming in behind him? Yes, I'm jealous and *I still get jealous* when someone beats me at anything, especially as I try so hard to follow the rules and to do it right and properly; the way it has always been done."

Emily: "You get beaten all the time because you don't like to *experiment* with new ideas or use your *imagination* to change old ideas that have been put to one side.

The best thing to be is a person who can say to themselves while they are doing something different "*Are you havin' any fun?*" You have to enjoy what you are doing and laugh through the mistakes you make.

I know that you are in the dance competition after the parade, what are you dancing?"

Georgia: "*The Jitterbug* with *Burt Collins* and the *Valentino Tango* with *Bill Bailey*. I can't seem to keep the timing right on both dances. Burt said to me "If *I concentrate on you* and the Jitterbug, then I won't be able to practice my second routine with Barbie. *Barbie's back* after winning her heat at the Nationals."

Lorraine: "I bet that *at this moment,* you could *cry me a river* because you are so frustrated and nervous.

Emily is right, if you start practicing *everyday* and you start making mistakes, then calm yourself down, think about what you are doing and ask yourself "*Are you having any fun?*" and if you believe you're not, then you shouldn't be dancing.

Competition dancing is serious business but it is also fun; dancing is fun and when you relax, the moves will flow from you easily.

I've got five dollars that says,

if you try what we have suggested, *come Saturday morning* you will be able to dance both dances without thinking about them."

Emily: "I'm going to get another coffee. Do either of you want another one? And *please don't talk about me when I'm gone.*"

Lorraine: "*There is always one more time* for you to practice *while the music plays* on and get your routines down pat. Just try what we have suggested, *this is all I ask.*"

A few minutes later, Emily returned with her coffee.

Emily: "The waitress just told me that Mrs. Jones was in here two weeks ago and told her that the man who lives across the road from her said that he wants to *take her to the Mardi Gras.*

She told her "Up *until yesterday,* he wouldn't speak

to me. He thinks that I have gone from *rags to riches* and now he wants to get to know me."

She also told me that *as time goes by* and *some kind of wonderful* happens, you soon find out who your real friends are. They are the ones who were there for you in the bad times and they don't want anything from you when the good times come to you."

Lorraine: "*The best thing is to be a person* who is a friend and accepts you for who you are and not what you've got.

You didn't know me when I was growing up in San Francisco but you have stuck by me since I have come to live here.

After coming back from visiting my parents and when I feel that *I left my heart in San Francisco,* the both of *you could make me smile again."*

Emily: "The waitress also told me that Mrs. Jones said to her "*I guess I'll have to change my plans* for the future. *At this moment,* I feel that since the pilot took off and never came back, I'm living in *a lonely place* and I *cry me a river* every night but *I wanna be loved* and *I wanna be around people* who won't give me the *next door blues*.

The man from across the road told her "*I'm an old cow hand from the Rio Grand* and I have retired up here because *I'm the king of broken hearts*. The females down there used to say to me *with plenty of money and you could fly me to the moon*. I say *congratulations to someone* who ends up with the woman who has the *cold, cold heart*. I have watched you struggling over the years but I didn't know how to approach you in a way that didn't look like you would have your *love for sale* to me."

Georgia: "*I wish I were in love again* but I think that *while we're young,* we should live our lives and go *dream dancing* if we want to.

Some people *marry young* and they live *nowhere with love* and are happy, where others, who *marry young* find that after awhile *something was missing* in their relationship and *somewhere along the way,* they ask themselves "*Where did the magic go?*" and they end up either playing the game *Charade* or *change partners* and hoping they will find the *crazy love* that they were looking for in *the second time around.*"

Emily: "I think I know the man who Mrs. Jones was talking about. I think that he was the school bus driver when I was at school.

People used to stand near the bus stop of the school preaching "*Sing you sinners,* don't be a *silly dreamer* under the *old devil moon.*

You won't be a *stranger in paradise,* the paradise that the Lord has for you once you repent your sins. You can live on the *street of dreams* if you would just *sing you sinners."*

We used to say "*Please driver,* would you let us out, just down the road away from these people."

But he replied "The *rules of the road* say that for your safety, I can only let you off the bus at the designated stops. I will report them to the school authorities and see if they can be moved on".

Georgia: "I remember one day, *Stella by starlight* stood there listening to them and when they said "*Sing you sinners.*" she did, she sang *Makin' Whoopee* and when they had stopped preaching *Stella by starlight* said "*Play it again, Sam* so that I can sing again."

She also told them one day, to go preach and sing *the Christmas song* to *the lonely goatherd* and be a *stranger in paradise,* their paradise and while you're there, you can *climb ev'ry mountain* with the goats."

They were not very impressed with her, but that was our Stella."

Emily: "Evidently, Mrs. Jones told the waitress that she said to the man across the road "*I can't believe that you're in love with me,* or so you say.

This *can't be love* because *you don't know me*. You have most probably heard all the talk that's been going around about me."

He said to her "I don't listen to gossip, I only believe what I see and *the shadow of your smile* tells me a lot about you. *You don't know me* either and *you didn't know me when* I was younger but we can start to get to know each other slowly, if you want to."

Georgia: "What did she say back to him?"

Emily: "I will have to think about it. *Taking a chance on love* is a big step for me. I did meet someone else while I was on holiday but he was impatient and wanted me to make decisions immediately. He flies all over *this funny world* so how many other females has he got in other countries that he consorts with.

You can *call me irresponsible* if I did make a decision without thinking about it, especially if it ended up being the wrong decision. I will have to think about what you have told me. Please give me a chance to do that, *this is all I ask.*"

Lorraine: "What would he have heard about her?"

Georgia: "He would have heard people saying that *the lady is a tramp*.

Somewhere along the way she had a brief encounter with a man with a *cold, cold heart* and she ended the relationship but he became nasty and started telling every one that *the lady is a tramp*.

He went to see her a few weeks later and said to her "I'm sorry, please *take me back again.*" but she told him to go away and leave her alone. She told him "Because of you, *I'm thru with love.*"

He went over a few more times to her place and every time she spoke to him she told him the same thing "*I'm through with love.*"

The last time he was there he said to her "If I can't get what I want from you; then I have *Georgia on my mind* and maybe she'll give me what I want."

Mrs. Jones said to him "*It's alright with me;* your kind of love *maybe* alright for her *but not for me.* I don't want you coming back here anymore."

And now Mrs. Jones just *don't get around much anymore.*"

Lorraine: "Oh my goodness, that man; that man across the road; that's *Captain Shaker.* He owns the *Thou Swell* Company in San Francisco.

Dad introduced me to him at

Ca C'est L' Amour Club's *Moondance* that raises money for diabetic research and we danced the *waltz for Debby* in memory of his late wife.

His company makes the *Thou Swell* Confectionary, the *Thou Swell* Biscuits but *Thou Swell* is better known for all their Diabetic products.

He doesn't need to spend much time at the company these days, but I wonder what he is doing here in town."

Georgia: "That man across the road with the hat on; is that the one you're talking about?"

Lorraine: "Yes, I'm sure he's dad's friend. He might be here for the *Bourbon Street Parade* on Saturday. When I speak to dad next, I'll have to tell him that I've seen him here."

Georgia: "That's the man who lives across the road from Mrs. Jones.

He was our school bus driver when I was at school.

They say that he moved here from the country and bought a house half way down *the Boulevard Of Broken Dream* and he has lived here for years.

I do remember that he used to go away for a few weeks, about every three months. Are you sure that's your dad's friend?"

Lorraine: "Yes, I'm sure. He owns the *Thou Swell* Company in San Francisco.

Dad was also telling me that very soon the *Thou Swell* Company will be bringing out a new line for diabetics called *Begin The Beguine*.

It has taken him two years to come up with a diabetic ice-cream and now he has done it and it's the beginning for some diabetics to be able to eat ice-cream for the first time which is why it's going to be called *Begin The Beguine*.

Dad told me that he lost his first wife to complication brought on by eating something that affected her diabetes."

Georgia: "Fancy that; a man that has gone from *rags to riches* living here; but why in that street?

You would think that he would have moved into a classier part of town. I wonder if Mrs. Jones knows his *rags to riches story.*"

Emily: "I doubt it. I don't think anyone knows, because if they did, then he would have people chasing him all the time for his money.

I don't think they we should tell anyone else about what we know.

Lorraine; *it had to be you,* didn't it. You had to see and

recognize him.

Just *think of how it's gonna be* when Mrs. Jones and the rest of the town finds out. I think once they do find out, *there'll be some changes made* to his life."

Lorraine: "Dad told me that he once asked the Captain, "Why did he move away from San Francisco?" and the Captain replied "I woke to *a foggy day,* everyday, *since my love has gone* and I always know when the *end of May* is coming, because *here comes that heartache again.*

I bought a house in the country because *it's so peaceful in the country* but it was too peaceful for me. *Give me the simple life* but give me somewhere where my *heartache tonight* won't feel as bad.

I left my heart in San

Francisco when I started travelling after Debby died and *since my love has gone, anywhere I wander* now, I see *what a wonderful world* we live in because *I used to be color blind* to it and didn't really see it.

Once upon a time and *once there lived a fool* who thought only of making money and living what he thought *the good life* was, but he found that the *good life* was not what he had.

I walk a little faster these days *by myself* but I see more than I used to and that's why I say "Just *give me the simple life"* and I *don't get around much any more.*
I still have fond memories of Debby and *they can't take that away from me* no matter who comes into my life in the future."

Emily: "Ah! That makes sense now. The waitress told me that "*Me and Mrs. Jones* ran into each other just the other day and she told me that she said to Shaker Brown, "I have thought about it very carefully and *my heart tells me* that *all of me* would like to start *taking a chance on love* with you but I must be honest from the start; *I can't give you anything but love* because I'm not rich like you might have heard and I feel that *you could make me smile again.*

You don't know what love is until you don't have it and it's true when they say "*You're nobody till somebody loves you.*" Still, *I can't believe that you're in love with me* but *the shadow of your smile* tells me that it's true."

Then she said his reply was "I told you that I don't listen to

89

gossip. *There'll be no more teardrops tonight* for you, once I tell you about me.

Oh, Marie, now it can be told; I am Captain Shaker, owner of the *Thou Swell* Company. *For once in my life,* and *because of you,* I am *feeling good*. Never do *I fall in love too easily;* until I met you and *the beat of my heart* became stronger and stronger. I have written you many *love letters* over the years but I have never posted them to you because *I left my heart in San Francisco* quite a few years ago.

Three weeks ago, I took a *sentimental journey* into my past and realized that *it's time* for me to move on and start living again. I also realized that *there's a lull in my life* that needs to be filled.

You go to my head and I

know that *you'd be so nice to come home to* both *night and day*. Also; *because of you* I see that *life is beautiful* and *life is a song,* so *let's face the music and dance* together and I won't ever do the *waltz for Debby* again unless you want me to. You must promise me, that you will always *save the last dance for me.*

Now let's give the other people in the street the *blues in the night* when they find out about you and me. This will give them something to gossip about; especially about me."

Georgia: "I bet that a lot of people living along *the Boulevard Of Broken Dreams* will be saying "*This can't be love* between them because *until yesterday* they hardly knew each other.

He will soon be saying to her "*You took advantage of me* because you found out that I

have gone from *rags to riches,*
even though I live opposite
you in a small plain house."

Emily: "*Isn't it romantic? For once
in my life* I believe that love
can be better *the second time
around* and I hope that it is for
them but *where do you go
from love* if it doesn't work
out."

Georgia: "I wonder if Santa would
bring me the man of my
dreams if I write it on my
grown-up Christmas list.

My parents keep telling us
children to *have a good time
while we're young* and not let
that *old devil moon* change our
recipe for love when we are
ready to *let there be love.*

Lorraine, what time did you
say that you had to be at the
Harronymous Theatre because
it's nine thirty now?"

Lorraine: "I'll have to go now. Are you
girls coming to the parade?

And Georgia, don't forget to ask yourself when you're dancing "*Are you havin' any fun?*" and I hope you will be."

Emily: "Yes, I am. So *somewhere along the way, I'll be seeing you* up on the float and I hope you have a *good shine* on your shoes because everyone will notice otherwise. Bye Lorraine."

Georgia: "I'll be down by the *Slow Interlude* Dance Hall with the others in the dance group. Maybe we can catch up after the competitions. Bye Lorraine."

Lorraine: "*I'll be around* at the *Blue and Sentimental* Hotel on Saturday evening so, *till then* have fun."

NEW TO TOWN

Sweet Lorraine left and Moonglow left a few minutes afterwards. I turned to Harry and said "Harry, you can wake up now, Moonglow has gone."

Harry opened one eye and said "*Oh, didn't he ramble on*. He sent me to sleep and *it had to be you,* who had to wake me. I was in the middle of *my reverie* with Miss *Solitaire.*

We were eating *Lofty's Roach Soufflé* at a place in *just a little street where old friends meet,* when it began to snow. Miss Solitaire called out *let it snow! let it snow! let it snow!* so we can go *shaking the blues* away if we have any after that delicious meal."

I looked at Harry and said "Your what? *You go to my head* and sometimes *I get a kick out of you* when you use those big words. Where do you get them from? *When Joanna loved me,* sometimes she used to use big words as well. She used to tell me what they meant but I've forgotten most of them now."

"*My reverie.*" said Harry "it means daydreaming. I hear others use big words and I find out what they mean and then use them myself.

Last week I heard *Laura* down by the *Twist & Shout* Hotdog vender *speak low* to *Maria Elena* and she said "*I left my heart in San Francisco* with *my funny Valentine.*

I met Valentine at the *Muskrat Ramble* Park. He was with the *Mountain Greenery* Circus and he was so comical; which is another word for funny.

He was always telling others that *you're never fully dressed without a smile* and to try *this funny world experiment; smile* at someone you pass in the street and watch their reaction. *Little did I dream* that *my funny Valentine* could make just about anybody *smile.*

My romance with *my funny Valentine* was brief because we had to come home but *my reverie* of him is still there and *they can't take that away from me.*" and that's where I got that word from.

Hey what's the commotion about? Look there's Quando, I wonder if he knows? Hey, *Quando, Quando, Quando,* what's going on?

I haven't seen so much excitement here since *maybe September* last year when the *Lullaby Of Broadway* Vaudeville Show was coming to town and all the females were running around talking about it and saying "*Happiness is a thing called Joe,* the main attraction. You can put him at the top of my *grown-up Christmas list* and I'll help him get over any *growing pains,* if he has some."

Quando said "There's a new gal in town and *wait till you see her* and her *angel eyes.*

She looks so *heavenly* in her short *blue velvet* coat. She could *fly me to the moon* and back and then *over the rainbow* that's *east of the sun* that we could have on *a rainy day* during an *Indian summer.*"

Harry replied "I know I *don't get around much anymore* but no-one could be that beautiful."

Quando said "I would *speak low* if I were you because here she comes and you can see for yourself."

"Hello, my name is *Stardust* and *I'm lost again*. I am supposed to be meeting my friend, Miss Jones near here. Have you seen her?" said *Stardust*.

"My name is Harry and this is Danny Boy. Did you say you were a friend of Miss Jones?" said Harry.

"Yes." said *Stardust* "I live opposite her. I came here from San Francisco, just two months ago and one day when I was out, I knew that *I was lost, I was drifting* along different streets looking for my place when Miss Jones ran into me and showed me the way home.

Oh, Danny Boy, your leg; what happened?"

"I was out walking with Joanna, when a driver with a *cold, cold heart* hit us and didn't stop. *I'm just a lucky so and so* because I had a few bad injuries but Joanna was killed. *At this moment,* because of the injuries, I *don't get around much anymore.*" I replied.

"Well, *if I ruled the world,* I would make it mandatory for anyone who doesn't obey the *rules of the road* and causes an accident that injures or kills others that they get locked up for the crime and they throw away the key." *Stardust* said and then she saw Miss Jones coming her way and said "*Have you met Miss Jones?"*

Stardust said "Hello, Miss Jones. I was looking for you as *I'm lost again.* I was asking Harry and Danny Boy, if they had seen you passing by. Harry and Danny Boy *haven't met you yet* so let me introduce them to you.

Danny Boy was hit by a car recently. We will have to get together one day soon Danny Boy and have a good chat."

I replied 'Yes, that would be nice.

Just let me know *where or when* and I'll arrange to be there."

Miss Jones remarked "Danny Boy, I think you had better bring Harry with you to keep me company because *Stardust* will have to *take me* to wherever you're going to meet or she'll get lost and I'll have to go looking for her again."

As the two females walked away, Quando said "Harry; *forget the woman, the lady is a tramp*. Well, that's what the word on the street is."

Harry said "*Darn that dream* I just had. You're not wrong; Stardust is the *most beautiful girl in the world* and Danny, I think that she would love to get *lost in the stars* with you."

"Yeah! Right Harry. *It had to be you* to get your *pure imagination* working over time again. Now that you have finally met Miss Jones, are you still going to be dreaming of eating *Lofty's Roach Soufflé* with what's her name? Now that you've met Miss Jones; are you happy now?" I said

Harry thought for a moment and replied "Yes, but I still don't think that *the lady is a tramp. Once upon a time,* a few years back, she may have been forced to do something she didn't want to do and you know how gossip can grow and change from one mouth to another *as time goes by*.

Like you said earlier, it could just be girl talk that has been blown out of all proportion.

It's *never too late* to find out what the truth is, so I think that the best thing for me to do is carefully and honestly ask her, her side of the story. If I am able to get her side of the story then nobody can *call me irresponsible* for jumping to conclusions."

I replied "*It amazes me* just how differently you see things and *what a wonderful world* it would be if others were like you.

You are someone who would *wrap your troubles in dreams and dream them away* and you would stand by others, even a *stranger in paradise,* who was having a bad time and you would give *one last pitch* for getting them help. You would even *take the moment* to ask the angels to help them if you had to."

"*Have I told you lately* but *yesterday I heard the rain* down south caused a lot of flooding; so much that they had to cancel *Colomby Day* at *Do-Re-Mi Park*. I always thought that they still held it *come rain or come shine.*" said Harry, trying to change the conversation.

As I took another couple of mouthfuls of my drink, I thought "*When Joanna loved me;* I was the happiest male around and I knew that *we are in love.* Joanna, *when I lost you, someone turned the moon upside down* for me. I was no-one *until I met you* and you told me "*I left my heart in San Francisco* with my other family." yet you still fell in love with me and *because of you* I became the best I could be.

At the moment; I feel like *I'm the king of broken hearts* and *my heart won't say goodbye* to you but then *my heart tells me* that I should move on and start to live again."

A flash memory of Joanna's face passed through his mind and he heard her say to him "Yes, *I left my heart in San Francisco* but you stopped the *blues in the night* for me.

You'll never find another love like mine but your *days of love* are not over and *the best is yet to come*.

I have sent you the *most beautiful girl in the world* to love you and *no one will ever know* that *it was me* who arranged this and *it's alright with me*.

She has not come to take my place but she will give you *candy kisses* and some *crazy love*.

The *very thought of you* being on your own makes *the beat of my heart* slow down but you have *the right to love* again.

Once you asked "*How can you mend a broken heart?*" and now you will find the answer in Stardust because you can't mend a broken heart, all you have to do is learn to have faith and love again.

Although *I can't believe that you're in love with me* so much still, you have to let go of me and *I wish you love* with Stardust.

You will never have to say "*Who can I turn to?*" because *I'll be around* always to keep you safe.

For once in my life I am happy to say "*Congratulations to someone* who now has your love."

I have so many sweet and funny memories and *they can't take that away from me,* even here in *my blue heaven. This time the dream's on me* and it is a special *one for my baby.*"

As I became aware of Harry's voice I said "*I'll be seeing you* Joanna and thanks for all you have done for me."

Harry said "What was that you were saying. Were you talking to Joanna or saying something to me."

I replied "It doesn't matter. I'm *in a sentimental mood* at the moment. What were you calling me for?"

Harry said "*Have I told you lately* that at times you seem to be *out of this world.* Are you sure that you still don't have concussion or some sort of brain injury that is making you like this *silly dreamer* who has come from either *over the rainbow* or from *over the sun?*"

"Nah." I replied "I just had a memory of Joanna and realized that *there's a lull in my life* at the moment and I feel like *I'm the king of broken hearts.*

Because of you and your thinking; especially about Miss Jones, *I wish I were in love again. Sometimes I'm happy* just having my *solitude* but that's when I become a *silly dreamer.*

Is that who I think it is coming down the street?"

Harry gave a chuckle and said "*It had to be you,* to come out with something like that. Believe me, you are definitely not a *silly dreamer* anymore. Maybe it's *just one of those things* that can happen to us occasionally; however, I do know that you will *make someone happy* and I think it will be soon."

"*Mr. Spill,* it's been a long time since I've seen you. What brings you back here to this town?" I asked.

"I finally *got her off my hands* and I think that it was *just in time.*" he said "she was just getting too much for me too handle. *She's got it bad* and they say "*you always hurt the one you love.*" and she has; she's hurt me so much that

I left. Well, now I'm saying "*Ding dong the witch is dead* and gone from out of my life."

"Come on now, it couldn't have been all that bad, could it?" I asked.

"*Where do I begin?*" he replied "*last night when we were young,* so she would say, we had a perfect *love story* going, until the curtains and *stars fell on Alabama* Theatre during the *closing theme,* which was the *Spider-man theme* for the last time. The show I was in, played its last performance and finished completely.

Most of the performers became unemployed but not for me because from there, I got a role in the *Lullaby Of Broadway* Vaudeville show and I was able to bring her into the role by doing a *Moondance* with her under a *blue moon*. The *blue light, red light* section was supposed to be dancing through some *autumn leaves* but she wanted to *let it snow, let it snow, let it snow*. It was impossible to *let it snow, let it snow, let it snow* every night plus the snow would melt too quickly under the lights which also made it dangerous to dance through.

To start off with; we lived *nowhere with love* and *my romance* with her was good *when love was all we had* and *while the music plays on* we were able to keep *dancing in the dark*.

Our *Moondance* routine became a hit in the show, so we danced it according to the season and we had a name for each one. There was; *Once upon a Summertime* and we had a gentle *summer wind* blowing on us; *It might as well be Spring,* when *Spring is here,* we pretended that *Here's that Rainy Day* again, we also had an imitation *White Christmas* for winter and a *Foggy* Day or autumn leaves for autumn.

She became *my funny valentine* one year and I knew that *I've grown accustomed to her face* and that *this can't be love* that I was feeling for her.

After our *White Christmas* routine was finished one night, the *Lullaby Of Broadway* cast were given two weeks off while we were in San Francisco and I had *Georgia on my mind* because I told my parents "*I'll be home for Christmas* that year."

We had a big argument because she didn't want go and meet my parents. I tried to reassure her by saying they would love her even though *they haven't met you yet,* but she still wouldn't come because she wanted to stay in the big smoke and *have a good time.*

I left my heart in San Francisco and went back to Georgia to visit my folks for a week, but when I went back to San Francisco I was told that she had gone away with a *candy man* the very afternoon that I had left.

She was very surprised to see that I had come back early from seeing my folks and began to *cry me a river* of tears for not being honest with me. The real reason for her not going with me was that she was meeting the new sponsors of the show; *The Valentino Tango* Biscuit Company.

The *Lullaby Of Broadway* Vaudeville show ran two more seasons but the crowds started to drop off and that meant the money wasn't coming in, so the show closed. The head of *The Valentino Tango* Biscuit Company wanted to *take her to the Mardi Gras* but she said she wouldn't go without me.

She told him that *we are in love* and that our *love is here to stay*.

Even though I didn't want to go to the Mardi Gras, I still went with her and while we were down there, she was offered the lead role in the new show *When Do The Bells Ring For Me* and I knew that she would do *what ever it takes* to get the lead.

My heart stood still when she told me that she had got the part but unfortunately I was not going to star opposite her. They wanted me to be the choreographer and teach our dance steps and routines to other cast members.

When Do The Bells Ring For Me had a few hitches to begin with because a few males, who were being auditioned for the lead, were unable to dance with her. *The other hours* that she was not in rehearsals she would say to me "*The shadow of your smile* tells me that you are disappointed that you are not starring opposite me. You know that *you go to my head* and *we are in love* and *that's all that matters*.

Please my love; be happy and supportive of me. *I've got you under my skin* and when I'm with you, *I've got the world on a string* but *tender is the night* tonight so *shall we dance* our *September Song while the music plays on*."

I replied to her "*The way you look tonight* and *the shadow of your smile* makes me believe that *we are in love* and I'm *lucky to be me* and the one that you love. *Baby, dream your dream* because *all I do is dream of you* succeeding and I'm right there by your side. *Just kiss me* and in our *love scene,* let me be your *lover* and *let there be love* between us for many years to come.

I knew that *she belongs to me* and our *recipe for love* was set because *my baby just cares for me,* or so I thought. Every time I kissed her, little did I know that she was *kissing a fool,* and that was me?"

I could write a book on what happened after that. *Darn that dream* I had of her making it in the big time because it really happened for her. She started to get *love letters* from her fans and that's when her fame went to her head. She became very demanding and *time after time* she had the *undecided blues* about what she really wanted.

One day she said to me "*Who can I turn to* these days when I want to get something done? *If I ruled the world* and I wanted something, it would mean that *I want it now, come rain or come shine,* it would have to be given to me right then."

I became angry and replied "Just take a look at yourself and see what you have become and *how insensitive* you are towards others. Receiving those *love letters* has your *pure imagination* working overtime. *Once upon a time* you could *fly me to the moon* but now you have become a monster with a *cold, cold heart* and I don't really want to be around you or be part of your world anymore."

She just said coldly "Well, *the party's over* for you then and *the day you leave me* won't *come by me* soon enough. It will be *congratulations to someone* else who gets involved with you.

I won't be saying "*Here comes that heartache again.*" but you will be saying "*How can you mend a broken heart?*" once you start missing me.

When you come crawling to me begging your *one last pitch* "*Please my love,* I'm sorry. Please *take me back again.*" all I will say is "*How do you say auf weidersehen.*" as *I'm walking* away."

One *lazy afternoon, Moon Indigo,* a playwright and director, approached me and asked me if I would like to be the choreographer and lead male in his new show *I'm Always Chasing Rainbows* that was opening, *maybe September* on Broadway. *For once in my life,* my talents were being recognized, so I accepted the role *zealously.*

When Do The Bells Ring For Me closed early due to the other cast members walking out because of *Mary Ruth*'s attitude and demands and she went into lesser roles and then into making Commercials.

I'm always Chasing Rainbows ran for three seasons on Broadway.

Mood Indigo decided to join up with another company to cast a musical called "*How Do You Keep The Music Playing*." The only song in the musical that was any good was *the Christmas song* and only after one season, *How Do You Keep The Music Playing* closed.

I heard that Mood Indigo had better success with his own musical, *I Gotta Right To Sing The Blues* and that he wanted me to do the choreography for it. *Since my love has gone* from dancing, I left San Francisco but I never *left my heart in San Francisco*."

"But what are you doing back here?" I asked.

Mr. Spill replied "I have *Georgia on my mind* again and since I told my folks that

I'll be home for Christmas, I thought that I might just as well move back home for a while so I've come to pack up."

"Have you heard any more about Mary Ruth?" I asked.

"Yeah, she's supposed to be around these parts looking for some fool to play opposite her. *Congratulations to someone* who is going to become her next victim.

Once there lived a fool in me who believed it would be *nice 'n' easy* to work with her; but it's just a matter of *he loves and she loves* until the *days of wine and roses* starts getting stale with her and she says "*I'll be seeing you* around sometime."

She never lets others work with her for too long and if she keeps that up, it won't be long before they drop her completely and go with someone new."

Harry looked at me and asked "Who are you talking about?"

I replied "It's better that you don't know."

Mr. Spill looked at Harry and then back to me and said "I think *I'll go* before I *cry me a river* with laughter. *I'll be seeing you."*

Harry began to get a bit angry and said "I want an answer to my question and *I want it now."*

"Okay, I'll tell you, but first listen to what I have to say." I said "remember you are only going for an audition and not *taking a chance on love*. The one that Mr. Spill and I have been talking about was Mary Ruth; Miss *Solitaire."*

"*Jeepers Creepers,* Danny. I don't think that I want the part now so *I guess I'll have to change my plans*. Instead of giving the *best of me,* I think that I'll take it as it comes and maybe not so willing to do things that they ask me to do.

Maybe finding out about what she can be like, could be *just in time* for me to think if show biz is what I want; besides the biscuits are not really that nice and I'll soon get sick of them." Harry said.

"Now *hold on* there. You have just heard a story about Mary Ruth and you believe it but what about the stories about Miss Jones.

You are giving her the chance to tell her side of the story so shouldn't you give Miss Solitaire the same opportunity to explain her side of the story?" I said.

"I suppose you're right. *It had to be you* to point this out to me. *Have I told you lately,* just what a good friend you are. I know that with Miss Jones, *I've grown accustomed to her face* and *I wanna be around her* for a long time to come; that is if she'll have me." Harry said.

We sat there quietly for a minute taking in the morning sun's warmth.

Then Harry said "Well, what do you think of Stardust, she is beautiful and I'm positive that she has an interest in you.

The *very thought of you* and her *taking a chance on love* would be *out of this world*. I don't think Joanna would mind; in fact, I think that she would think of *how sweet it is* that you are not moping around over her anymore."

THE ANSWERS

As I finished my drink I thought "*Since my love has gone, nobody's heart belongs to me* and *my heart won't say goodbye* to Joanna but I should really make the effort to move on. *I thought about you* Joanna; Harry is right when he says that *all I do is dream of you* but what would happen if *I fall in love too easily?*

I wish I were in love again and *I wanna be loved* by someone but *I've got you under my skin* still and *it don't mean a thing* if I *just say I love her* and tell her that *I can't give you anything but love.*

Oh Joanna, *you're all the world to me* so why did *it had to be you* to die on that awful day, is something I'll never understand. I also think that Harry is right when he says that I may still have some concussion and if he is right, *who can I turn to* for help?

Why does it have to be me to feel like a *stranger in paradise* and walk around with *a foggy day here in my heart* every day?

For once in my life I feel like *all of me* wants to give up and come and join you up there because *you could make me smile again* and seeing that I *don't get around much anymore,* no one will ever know I'm gone."

Then in my head I heard "*Don't be a baby, baby* because you know that is the wrong way of thinking. Even *a foggy day in London town* is blown away quickly and then the comments are "*Isn't it a lovely day* to *wrap your troubles in dreams* to dream away."

Once upon a time there was this feller who showed a *lonely girl* that *life is a song* so *let's face the music and dance.* Like that *song for you, so beats my heart for you* but all I can do for you now is to *light the way* for you towards a new life with a new love.

I know that if I was the lucky one and *if you were mine,* I would let *that crazy little thing called love* take over my *body* and soul and I would *always let there be love* for you.

As I told you earlier, I have sent Stardust, *all for you* to love and she will love you, even more than I did, in return. So *let's begin* to get back to the Danny that I loved. I *don't like goodbyes* so I will stay near you but in a *heavenly* way and I won't interfere with your life. Don't ever ask "*Who can I turn to?*" because you will know that I'm near and so are many other angels who will help you.

Just believe that *somewhere along the way, the shadow of your smile* will brighten another heart and that will make them smile.

So *don't cry baby,* not for me anymore, *this is all I ask* because *I wish you love.* Now *softly as I leave you,* you must promise me now, that you won't cry anymore and that you will give Stardust a chance."

"I promise. *I won't cry anymore* for you and the next time I see Stardust I'll be wearing *the brightest smile in town.*" I whispered.

"Danny, Danny, snap out of it. Look, here comes Stardust again. What is it with her? I thought that you lost your sense of direction *as time goes by* and you get old, not *while we're young*.

Now *hold on,* is that a *shadow of your smile* that I'm seeing on your face or gas from drinking the rest of your drink too quickly.

Normally, *you go to my head* with your wisdom and stories but *I can't believe that you're in* such a strange mood today. One minute you're all talkative and the next minute you are quiet and gloomy." said Harry.

"*I'm lost again.*" said Stardust.

I said "Well, you had better stay here with us until Miss Jones comes along to take you back home."

"Thank you." she said "*I'm just a lucky so and so* to have two friends that I can rely on.

May I sit here beside you Danny, until Miss Jones gets here?"

Harry looked at both of us and said jokingly "Now *isn't it romantic,* you're both *close enough for love*. Mind that she doesn't try to *kiss you* Danny, there again if she did; I know that she wouldn't *be kissing a fool*.

Okay, now here comes your partner in crime Stardust."

"Oh, there you are Stardust. When I saw you get out, I had a feeling where you were going. *I walk a little faster* than you usually do but I couldn't catch up this time." said Miss Jones.

"You know that I'm still trying to find my way around this place and I can't help it if I find that *I'm lost again*. I never have had a good sense of direction; it's *just one of those things*." said Stardust.

"And I suppose that it's *just one of those things* that you remembered where Harry and Danny were. Just *stay where you are,* that is, if it is alright with the fellers for us to stay until they are ready to leave. I'll just sit here by Harry." said Miss Jones.

Harry looked at me and happily said "*It's alright with me*. It would be nice to get to know each other better."

"Mr. Spill came past today and told us that he and Mary Ruth had split. He said that she was in town somewhere auditioning for a male, to star opposite her in her new commercial. Have you seen her around?" I asked.

Miss Jones replied "No, I haven't but I have heard the rumors and the gossip. Both of *these foolish things* can be blown out of all proportions and it can hurt whoever the gossips about.

Take me for instance; I was kidnapped and forced to do things that I'm ashamed of, but I had no choice but to do as I was told, because the kidnapper threatened to kill me otherwise. I was lucky that I was able to get away from the situation and get home.

Those memories are very hard to forget, but the short time I had with my son, is the good memory that I will always have and *they can't take that away from me. If I love again,* it will have to be special because I can't have anymore babies due to complications after having my son."

Stardust looked at her friend with tears in her eyes and said "Oh, Miss Jones I never knew about that; I just thought you liked the *solitude* of your family. Did they ever catch the mongrel that put you through all that?"

"No, they didn't. Now please don't tell anyone because *only you* know the true story.

Others will only say it's an excuse to cover up what they believe and I don't want to have to go through years of what I have already been through again.

I won't cry anymore over it and *the man that got away* with it." replied Miss Jones sadly.

Harry began to *speak low* and softly saying "I have heard the rumors and I was telling Danny earlier that I didn't believe them and if I ever met you, I was going to ask for the truth. You have told all of us here the truth and I can assure you that we won't say anything to others.

You are amongst real friends here and anytime you would like to have a chat, then *I wanna be around* for you and I would listen without judgment."

Miss Jones replied surprisingly "Why thank you Harry. Not many others are as understanding as you and *if I love again,* then I hope it would be to someone like you because I think that you would be *easy to love."*

Their conversation was interrupted by the sound of other voices talking loudly near them.

Waitress: "Guess what? *Me and Mrs. Jones* have just finished having lunch together and she has just told me that over dinner last night at a very expensive restaurant, Captain Shaker has asked her to move in with him but not in the house across the road.

He told her that *there's a small hotel* that he owns not far from here, on the posh side of town and the managers are going overseas so he intends to run it himself."

Emily: "How many properties does he own around here? If he's going to manager the hotel, that would mean that most of his time will be taken up with the business so what will he do in *the other hours* that he's not working?"

Waitress: "She told me that he said to her "Up *until I met you,* I often thought "*I wish I were in love again* and *I wished on the moon* for it to happen.

Then I saw you and knew that *if I love again,* it would have to be with a *sophisticated lady* who was down to earth. Well, once I had spoken to you, *love walked in* to my life and the *more I see you, all of me* would like to be your *lover* but *not as a stranger,* but as your husband."

Georgia: "You mean, he actually proposed to her. Well, that certainly is a *prelude to a kiss,* isn't it?"

Waitress: "She replied "But *I can't give you anything but love* and *all of me. It had to be you* to fall in love with me so quickly. I don't know what to say. *Please my love,* give me time to think about it, *this is all I ask.*"

Georgia: "What is she waiting for? If it was me, I would be saying yes now and I would not be having any *sleepless* nights over the decision.

The *recipe for love* can be changed and *no one will ever know* that it has been, except that *old devil moon. My romance* could grow into a very strong love after I've made him *all mine.*"

Emily: "A man with money; is that all you're interested in? Look at Laura Brown, she married a man with money and thought "*With plenty of money and you,* I could travel and have the best of everything." but all she got was the *bare necessities* because all the money was tied up in the *Wolverine Blues* Timber Industry.

He wouldn't even buy her a new *blue velvet* dress to go to a special dinner in. Money might be a part of what you want; *but not for me,* I would like just enough to live comfortably.

When I fall in love, *I wanna be around* a happy home and the *days of wine and roses* are special occasions and he can *just kiss me* to make *the beat of my heart* skip *two by two.*

I would know that *we are in love* and it won't just be *while we're young* but forever."

Waitress: "I agree with you Emily but *why do people fall in love* and then after a few years, they start having affairs. If they knew that *this can't be love* to start with, then why get married.

I knew a girl who got married and a year later she was having an affair with *the best man,* who was her husband's brother but to top it all off, her husband was having an affair with one of the bridesmaids. When his wife found out, all his excuse was "*I got lost in her arms* and I couldn't find my way out."

Georgia: "Did he really tell his wife that "*I got lost in her arms* and couldn't get out."

That's a new one that I'll have to use sometime.

I told someone once "*All I do is dream of you* under the *blue moon.*" but I was seven at the time and it was just after my father had said "*Come fly with me* while we still have *blue skies* because the forecast is for rain later today.

Dad then said "*I get a kick out of you* but it will be *congratulations to someone* who will be the lucky one to take you away from me.

Dad's favorite saying to me when I was young was "*I get a kick out of you.*" and he still says it sometimes when I talk to him."

Emily: "That's a bit like something Lorraine told me whenever she had to leave home to go back to the Music Conservatory.

She told her father that whenever he listened to his favorite piece of music that he would "*Hear me in the harmony.*" and know that I still loved him.

She actually learnt the piece of music and played it to him one day when she was home for the holidays and her father said to her mother "*Because of you,* we have a very beautiful and talented daughter so *let's face the music and dance* to the piece she is playing."

Talking about dance;, how are your routines going Georgia?"

Waitress: "Are you in the dance competition next Saturday? What are you dancing?"

Georgia: "Yes I'm dancing the Jitterbug and the Valentino Tango and *because of you* Emily and Lorraine, I have really improved in both routines and can go *all the way* through without making any mistakes.

Did Mrs. Jones tell you what she intends to do about her proposal?"

Waitress: "She said "To start with, *my heart stood still* when he said he wanted to be my *lover* until he finished his sentence with the proposal. It was the rest of the conversation that made me think harder because he said "I know that *I left my heart in San Francisco* after my wife's death and her memory, well, *they can't take that away from me* but *I only have eyes for you* now.

I *can't help falling in love* with you because there's *something in your smile* that tells me that *you'd be so nice to come home* to every night. They say that *you're nobody till somebody loves you* and they're right.

You'll never know what you have done to me and I promise that *you'll never find another love like mine*. You bring out the *best of me* and I can't wait to make *all of you all mine*. I will be *a weaver of dreams* and make every one of yours come true.

Don't cry baby, for once in my life I know what I want and I want you. Yes, *I mean you* because *baby, you've got what it takes* to make me happy.

Come on; *put your head on my shoulder* until your tears stop and then *let's face the music and dance* the rest of the night away. *Life is a song* so *let's begin* to sing it but you always have to *save the last dance for me.* Now let's have a drink.

"Waitress, two glasses of your best Champagne please; one for me and *one for my baby.*"

She said that she told him "*When I look in your eyes* and *the shadow of your smile* tells me that you are sincere and that *you could make me smile again.*

Your *recipe for love* is certainly unique and I have found that when I *kiss you,* I'm not *kissing a fool.*"

Georgia: "*Isn't it romantic* but did she accept his proposal? *They say it's wonderful* when someone proposes to you. I would be in quite a bit of bother if that was me, because *I fall in love too easily* and I would be getting engaged nearly every weekend.

Dad always said that *while we're young,* we should live a bit but *where do you start*. There are so many things I want to do and so many places I want to visit and *have a good time* in.

Sometimes I think *I could write a book* but *I can't stop* long enough for me to figure out what I'm doing the following day, let alone sit and write."

Emily: "I believe that somewhere in your *beautiful madness* there would be time to write but at the moment; with you, *anything goes*.

As time goes by, you will settle down and then you will be able to get your life in order but don't become predictable like *Nancy* because she should be *'long about now* and she will go into that shop to buy the paper. There she goes, into the shop and now she's leaving with her paper.

Now did Mrs. Jones tell you her decision or not. Is she going to get married?"

Waitress: "Well, she did say that when he took her home, it was in a limo and he said to the driver "*Please driver, take the long way back past my hotel so that Mrs. Jones can see where she could be living.*

I just can't believe *the way you look tonight* because you are so beautiful. *Tender is the night* so *put your head on my shoulder* and just relax there for a moment. Just *stay where you are* until I tell you to look at your new home; if you decide to marry me."

When he told her to look,

she saw this very elegant building that didn't look like a hotel; in fact, the hotel was next door and he said to her "The house is the manager's living quarters and we would be living in there.

The hotel has very experienced staff, so I would only be spending between two to four hours, three times a week there. The *other hours* would be spent in any way you wished to spend them.

There is also a special room with a garden for Stardust and possibly Miss. Jones as well. I doubt that *there'll be some changes made* to accommodate them except for adding an extra large cushion bed for Miss. Jones."

She responded by saying

"I can see that I could have *some kind of wonderful* life living here with you, but I need to be sure before I make my decision. I need to be sure that *we are in love* because all the material trimmings that you are offering are very tempting but *it don't mean a thing* if the love's not there.

I know that *you're nobody till somebody loves you* and I told myself years ago "*If I love again, the second time around* would be completely different to the first time and *because of you,* I know that it would be.

Please my love, allow me a little more time to think, *this is all I ask.* I will give you my decision before we part tonight."

Miss. Jones looked at Harry and asked "Do you always go around dressed like that? I don't want to seem to be rude, but you do look ridiculous."

Harry blushed and said "No. I am going to audition for the commercial with Miss Solitaire. I had a dream last night that I got the role but *darn that dream* because I don't know now if I want to do it."

Stardust said "If you really want the part, *just say I love her* but to someone who is standing near her? Make sure she hears you so don't *speak low* and when the *intro* is signaled; just give her a wink and a big *smile. These foolish things* are what she likes; *she's funny that way.*

You didn't know me when I was younger but Mary Ruth and I used to hang out together until she got into show business and was doing very well.

Then she became a big star and she changed into some sort of monster. It is becoming a problem for the company to keep her leading men, due to her demands.

I could write a book on her and a few other stars that I know, but hers would be the most interesting and the most damaging for her career. I don't blame you if you are having second thoughts of doing the audition."

Danny said "*I could write a book* as well, like a lot of others but not many of them take the time to do it, and if they did, would it be very interesting for others to read. I am not the reading type, so why should I take the time to write when there's a possibility that no one will read it."

Miss. Jones said "We can talk about that another time but I do think that Stardust and I should be getting home. *Stay where you are,* don't get up and Harry, remember *anything goes* in show biz and if you don't get this role, then it's *just one of those things* and *there is always one more time* to try out especially while *we're young.*"

"Yes." said Stardust "good luck or rather as they say in the theatre, break a leg and don't take any nonsense from Miss. Solitaire as she likes to be called these days.

But if she does try to give you trouble, just say to her "*Yesterday I heard the rain* say it's one of those *yellow days* that you can *wrap your trouble in dreams.*"

That will give her a shock because she knows what it means. It was also something very private between us and she will be less likely to cause you any trouble because she knows that she will have to deal with me if she does."

Harry said "Thank you both for your support and Miss. Jones, if I don't get the role then remember that I'll always be here if you ever say to yourself again "*Who can I turn to* for a chat?"

I said "Emily and Georgia have been so engrossed with whatever they have been talking about, that they didn't even notice the females here with us and *for once in my life,* I'm glad that I *don't get around much anymore.*

I know I keep saying *I wish I were in love again* but I have this strange feeling for Stardust and it's just like the one I had for Joanna. *This can't be love* that's happening to me, can it?"

"I am having some warm feelings for Miss. Jones so *if this can't be love,* then I would like to know what it is because it is making me feel warm all over.

I have been thinking about the *last night when we were young* and that Scottish lassie that I had a thing for and when she went back to Scotland, I thought that *I'll never smile again* and *where do you go from love* that is torn away from you?

You know what Danny; I think that *we are in love* with those two beautiful females. Georgia is going to *take me* to the audition and I know exactly what I'm going to do there." said Harry.

"What are you going to do Harry? I know by the tone in your voice that you are thinking of getting into mischief." I asked.

Emily: "Are you going to keep us in suspense or don't you know her decision. *It had to be you* that she has spoken to because you have to give every single little detail before you come to the conclusion.

Once upon a time, you never listened to what people had to say. You didn't want to know about anything that was going on; not even about a *stranger in paradise.*

But now, you know just about everything that's going on; all the *where or when* or whys and then when you get to a part that made *my heart stood still;* you still won't tell us what she replied."

Waitress: "How else am I going to spend *my time of day?*

Time after time, people come in here and tell me "*My romance* has ended or *my baby just cares for me.*"

Sometimes they expect me to answer questions like "*Who can I turn to* now, *since my love has gone?* or "*Why does it have to be me* and now *I'm lost again?*"

Emily: "Maybe it's *just one of those things* that becomes a part of your job, just like it can become a part of a bar attendant's job.

At least you help people while they're here because they need someone to talk to and *it had to be you* to be the one there for them, while in the *other hours* they might just be alone in their own little place. You never know that just by listening to them for a short while you maybe *just in time* to stop them from doing something foolish.

So what did she say?"

Waitress: "She said that when she got home that night she said to him "I have thought about this very seriously. *Tender is the night so beats my heart for you. Darn that dream* I had years ago because *it had to be you* and the *way you look tonight* that has made it hard for me not to say no too you; so, my answer is yes.

I thought that *this can't be love* that happening to me so quickly but I was finding myself getting lonely and I realized that it was *only 'cause I don't have you* and your love here with me."

She told me he said "You know that *you're nobody till somebody loves you* and that *you'll never get away from me* now. *Yesterday I heard the rain* tell me *what a wonderful world* we live in and that *some kind of wonderful* news is going to come to me soon. *Put your head on my shoulder* because with *the way you look tonight,* I don't want you to go, so stay with me for a while longer.

Now I would like you to think about the wedding; just

tell me *where or when* and I will take care of everything. I won't even care if it's in the garden of your new home when *spring is here* or when the *summer wind* blows gently off the river.

You said yes, and *that's all* that matters."

Georgia: "I knew that she would marry him.

Oh my goodness, look at the time. If I hurry, I'll get Harry to his audition *just in time*. *I've got five dollars* for parking and I'll call you later, *I've got your number*. Come on Harry."

Then Harry said "Listen to those girls gossiping about someone. We would never do that. Oh look, *sweet Georgia Brown* is ready to leave. I'll catch up with you tomorrow and let you know how I got on today."

"Yeah, ok." I said "good luck and don't take any nonsense from that Miss *Solitaire.*"

Emily looked down at me and said "Well *Danny Boy,* the vet said that you should be getting a bit more exercise for that leg, so let's go chase the ball around the park."

REFERENCE

MICHAEL BUBLÉ

MICHAEL BUBLÉ
CRAZY LOVE
CRY ME A RIVER
ALL OF ME
GEORGIA ON MY MIND
CRAZY LOVE
HAVEN'T MET YOU YET
ALL I DO IS DREAM OF YOU
HOLD ON
HEARTACHE TONIGHT
YOU'RE NOBODY TILL SOMEBODY LOVES YOU
BABY (YOU'VE GOT WHAT IT TAKES) (FEAT. SHARON JONES AND THE DAP-KINGS)
AT THIS MOMENT
STARDUST (FEAT. NATURALLY 7)
WHATEVER IT TAKES (FEAT. RON SEXSMITH, BONUS TRACK)
SOME KIND OF WONDERFUL (BONUS TRACK)

COME FLY WITH ME CD
NICE 'N EASY
CAN'T HELP FALLING IN LOVE
MY FUNNY VALENTINE
MACK THE KNIFE
FEVER
YOU'LL NEVER KNOW
FOR ONCE IN MY LIFE
MOONDANCE

MICHAEL BUBLÉ/LET IT SNOW CD
DISC1
FEVER
MOONDANCE
KISSING A FOOL
FOR ONCE IN MY LIFE
HOW CAN YOU MEND A BROKEN HEART
SUMMER WIND
YOU'LL NEVER FIND ANOTHER LOVE
LIKE MINE
CRAZY LITTLE THING CALLED LOVE
PUT YOUR HEAD ON MY SHOULDER
SWAY
THE WAY YOU LOOK TONIGHT
COME FLY WITH ME
THAT'S ALL

(BONUS MATERIAL) (NOT USED IN STORY)
DISC 2
LET IT SNOW! LET IT SNOW! LET IT SNOW!
THE CHRISTMAS SONG
GROWN-UP CHRISTMAS LIST
I'LL BE HOME FOR CHRISTMAS
WHITE CHRISTMAS

IT'S TIME CD
FEELING GOOD
FOGGY DAY, A (IN LONDON TOWN)
YOU DON'T KNOW ME
QUANDO, QUANDO, QUANDO
HOME
CAN'T BUY ME LOVE
MORE I SEE YOU
SAVE THE LAST DANCE FOR ME
TRY A LITTLE TENDERNESS
HOW SWEET IT IS
SONG FOR YOU
I'VE GOT YOU UNDER MY SKIN
YOU AND I
SOFTLY AS I LEAVE YOU (BONUS TRACK)

CRAZY LOVE CD
DISC 1:
CRY ME A RIVER
ALL OF ME
GEORGIA ON MY MIND
CRAZY LOVE
HAVEN'T MET YOU YET
ALL I DO IS DREAM OF YOU
HOLD ON
HEARTACHE TONIGHT
YOU'RE NOBODY TILL SOMEBODY LOVES YOU
BABY (YOU'VE GOT WHAT IT TAKES)
AT THIS MOMENT
STARDUST
WHATEVER IT TAKES
SOME KIND OF WONDERFUL
DISC 2:
HOLLYWOOD
AT THIS MOMENT
HAVEN'T MET YOU YET
END OF MAY
ME AND MRS. JONES
TWIST & SHOUT
HEARTACHE TONIGHT
BEST OF ME

MICHAEL BUBLÉ/LET IT SNOW CD
FEVER
MOONDANCE
KISSING A FOOL
FOR ONCE IN MY LIFE
HOW CAN YOU MEND A BROKEN HEART
SUMMER WIND
YOU'LL NEVER FIND ANOTHER LOVE
LIKE MINE
CRAZY LITTLE THING CALLED LOVE
PUT YOUR HEAD ON MY SHOULDER
SWAY
THE WAY YOU LOOK TONIGHT
COME FLY WITH ME
THAT'S ALL

BABALU CD
SPIDER-MAN THEME
YOU MUST HAVE BEEN A BEAUTIFUL
BABY
YOU'LL NEVER KNOW
LAZY RIVER
OH MARIE
CAN'T HELP FALLING IN LOVE
BILL BAILEY
BUENA SERA

WHEN YOU'RE SMILING
WHAT A WONDERFUL WORLD
DON'T GET AROUND MUCH ANYMORE
MACK THE KNIFE
VIE EN ROSE, LA

DREAM CD
DREAM
ANEMA E CORE
I'LL NEVER SMILE AGAIN
STARDUST
YOU ALWAYS HURT THE ONE YOU LOVE
DON'T BE A BABY, BABY
MARIA ELENA
DADDY'S LITTLE GIRL
PAPER DOLL
SURRENDER
TILL THEN
YOU BELONG TO ME
I WISH YOU LOVE

CRAZY LOVE
CRY ME A RIVER
ALL OF ME
GEORGIA ON MY MIND
CRAZY LOVE

HAVEN'T MET YOU YET
ALL I DO IS DREAM OF YOU
HOLD ON
HEARTACHE TONIGHT
YOU'RE NOBODY TILL SOMEBODY LOVES
YOU
BABY (YOU'VE GOT WHAT IT TAKES)
AT THIS MOMENT
STARDUST
WHATEVER IT TAKES

MICHAEL BUBLÉ CD ENHANCED CD
FEVER
MOONDANCE
KISSING A FOOL
FOR ONCE IN MY LIFE
HOW CAN YOU MEND A BROKEN HEART
SUMMER WIND
YOU'LL NEVER FIND ANOTHER LOVE
LIKE MINE
CRAZY LITTLE THING CALLED LOVE
PUT YOUR HEAD ON MY SHOULDER
SWAY
THE WAY YOU LOOK TONIGHT
COME FLY WITH ME
THAT'S ALL

CRAZY LOVE CD
CRY ME A RIVER
ALL OF ME
CRAZY LOVE
HAVEN'T MET YOU YET
ALL I DO IS DREAM OF YOU
HOLD ON
HEARTACHE TONIGHT
YOU'RE NOBODY TILL SOMEBODY
LOVES YOU
BABY (YOU'VE GOT WHAT IT TAKES)
AT THIS MOMENT
STARDUST
WHATEVER IT TAKES

HOLLYWOOD: THE DELUXE EP CD
HOLLYWOOD
AT THIS MOMENT
SOME KIND OF WONDERFUL
END OF MAY
ME AND MRS. JONES
HAVEN'T MET YOU YET
HEARTACHE TONIGHT
BEST OF ME

CRAZY LOVE CD SPECIAL EDITION
DISC 1:
CRY ME A RIVER
ALL OF ME
GEORGIA ON MY MIND
CRAZY LOVE
HAVEN'T MET YOU YET
ALL I DO IS DREAM OF YOU
HOLD ON
HEARTACHE TONIGHT
YOU'RE NOBODY TILL SOMEBODY LOVES YOU
BABY (YOU'VE GOT WHAT IT TAKES)
AT THIS MOMENT
STARDUST
WHATEVER IT TAKES
DISC 2:
HOLLYWOOD
AT THIS MOMENT
SOME KIND OF WONDERFUL
END OF MAY
ME AND MRS. JONES
HAVEN'T MET YOU YET
HEARTACHE TONIGHT
BEST OF ME

LET IT SNOW CD EXTENDED PLAY

LET IT SNOW! LET IT SNOW! LET IT SNOW!
THE CHRISTMAS SONG
GROWN-UP CHRISTMAS LIST
I'LL BE HOME FOR CHRISTMAS
WHITE CHRISTMAS
LET IT SNOW! LET IT SNOW! LET IT SNOW!

MICHAEL BUBLÉ (5 BONUS TRACKS)

FEVER
MOONDANCE
KISSING A FOOL
FOR ONCE IN MY LIFE
HOW CAN YOU MEND A BROKEN HEART
SUMMER WIND
YOU'LL NEVER FIND ANOTHER LOVE LIKE MINE
CRAZY LITTLE THING CALLED LOVE
PUT YOUR HEAD ON MY SHOULDER
SWAY
WAY YOU LOOK TONIGHT
COME FLY WITH ME
THAT'S ALL

LET IT SNOW, LET IT SNOW, LET IT
SNOW
CHRISTMAS SONG
GROWN-UP CHRISTMAS LIST
I'LL BE HOME FOR CHRISTMAS
WHITE CHRISTMAS

BIBLIOGRAPHY

CRAZY LOVE:
http://en.wikipedia.org/wiki/Michael_Bubl
%C3%A9_discography

COME FLY WITH ME CD:
http://en.wikipedia.org/wiki/Michael_Bubl
%C3%A9_discography

MICHAEL BUBLÉ/LET IT SNOW CD:
http://en.wikipedia.org/wiki/Michael_Bubl
%C3%A9_discography

IT'S TIME CD:
http://en.wikipedia.org/wiki/Michael_Bubl
%C3%A9_discography

CRAZY LOVE CD:
http://en.wikipedia.org/wiki/Michael_Bubl
%C3%A9_discography

MICHAEL BUBLÉ/LET IT SNOW CD:
http://en.wikipedia.org/wiki/Michael_Bubl
%C3%A9_discography

BABALU CD:
http://en.wikipedia.org/wiki/Michael_Bubl
%C3%A9_discography

DREAM CD:
http://en.wikipedia.org/wiki/Michael_Bubl
%C3%A9_discography

CRAZY LOVE CD:
http://www.cduniverse.com/productinfo.a
sp?pid=8402710

CRAZY LOVE CD:
http://www.cduniverse.com/productinfo.a
sp?pid=8402710

LET IT SNOW CD EXTENDED PLAY:
http://www.cduniverse.com/productinfo.a
sp?pid=8402710

HOLLYWOOD: THE DELUXE EP CD:
http://www.cduniverse.com/productinfo.a
sp?pid=8402710

MICHAEL BUBLÉ (5 BONUS TRACKS):
http://new.uk.music.yahoo.com/michael-buble/albums/michael-buble-5-bonus-tracks--22269656

HARRY CONNICK JNR

ELEVEN
SWEET GEORGIA BROWN
TIN ROOF BLUES
WOLVERINE BLUES
JAZZ ME BLUES
DOCTOR JAZZ
MUSKRAT RAMBLE
LAZY RIVER
JOE AVERY'S PIECE
WAY DOWN YONDER IN NEW ORLEANS

BLUE LIGHT, RED LIGHT
BLUE LIGHT, RED LIGHT (SOMEONE'S THERE)
A BLESSING AND A CURSE
YOU DIDN'T KNOW ME WHEN
JILL
HE IS THEY ARE
WITH IMAGINATION (I'LL GET THERE)
IF I COULD GIVE YOU MORE

THE LAST PAYDAY
IT'S TIME
SHE BELONGS TO ME
SONNY CRIED
JUST KISS ME

WE ARE IN LOVE
WE ARE IN LOVE
ONLY 'CAUSE I DONT HAVE YOU
RECIPE FOR LOVE
DRIFTING
FOREVER, FOR NOW
A NIGHTINGALE SANG IN BERKELEY
SQUARE
HEAVENLY
JUST A BOY
I'VE GOT A GREAT IDEA
I'LL DREAM OF YOU AGAIN
IT'S ALRIGHT WITH ME
BURIED IN BLUE

LOFTY'S ROACH SOUFFLE
ONE LAST PITCH
HUDSON BOMMER
LONELY SIDE
MR. SPILL

LOFTY'S ROACH SOUFFLE
MARY RUTH
HARRONYMOUS
ONE LAST PITCH (TAKE 2)
COLOMBY DAY
LITTLE DANCING GIRL
BAYOU MAHARAJAH

WHEN HARRY MET SALLY... MUSIC FROM THE MOTION PICTURE

IT HAD TO BE YOU (BIG BAND AND VOCALS)
LOVE IS HERE TO STAY
STOMPIN' AT THE SAVOY
BUT NOT FOR ME
WINTER WONDERLAND
DON'T GET AROUND MUCH ANYMORE
AUTUMN IN NEW YORK
I COULD WRITE A BOOK
LET'S CALL THE WHOLE THING OFF
IT HAD TO BE YOU (TRIO INSTRUMENTAL)
WHERE OR WHEN

20
AVALON
BLUE SKIES
IMAGINATION
DO YOU KNOW WHAT IT MEANS TO
MISS NEW ORLEANS?
BASIN STREET BLUES
LAZY RIVER
PLEASE DON'T TALK ABOUT ME WHEN
I'M GONE
STARS FELL ON ALABAMA
'S WONDERFUL
IF I ONLY HAD A BRAIN
DO NOTHIN' TILL YOU HEAR FROM ME

HARRY CONNICK, JR.
LOVE IS HERE TO STAY
LITTLE CLOWN
ZEALOUSLY
ON THE SUNNY SIDE OF THE STREET
I MEAN YOU
VOCATION
ON GREEN DOLPHIN STREET
LITTLE WALTZ
E

FRANCE I WISH YOU LOVE CD

BLUE LIGHT RED LIGHT
FOREVER FOR NOW
I WISH YOU LOVE
IT HAD TO BE YOU
DON'T GET AROUND MUCH ANY
ONE LAST PITCH
IT'S ALRIGHT WITH ME
BAYOU MAHARAJAH
DO YOU KNOW WHAT IT MEANS
RECIPE FOR LOVE
YOU DIDN'T KNOW ME WHEN
BUT NOT FOR ME
BLESSING & A CURSE
HEAVENLY
WITH IMAGINATION
WE ARE IN LOVE

COME BY ME/SONGS I HEARD CD
DISC 1

NOWHERE WITH LOVE
COME BY ME
CHARADE
CHANGE PARTNERS
EASY FOR YOU TO SAY
TIME AFTER TIME

NEXT DOOR BLUES
EASY TO LOVE
THERE'S NO BUSINESS LIKE SHOW
BUSINESS
A MOMENT WITH ME
DANNY BOY
CRY ME A RIVER
LOVE FOR SALE
DISC 2
SUPERCALIFRAGILISTICEXPIALIDOCIOU
S
THE LONELY GOATHERD
DING-DONG! THE WITCH IS DEAD
MAYBE
PURE IMAGINATION / CANDY MAN
PURE IMAGINATION / CANDY MAN
GOLDEN TICKET / I WANT IT NOW
GOLDEN TICKET / I WANT IT NOW
OOMPA LOOMPA
A SPOONFUL OF SUGAR
STAY AWAKE
SOMETHING WAS MISSING
YOU'RE NEVER FULLY DRESSED
WITHOUT A SMILE
OVER THE RAINBOW
THE JITTERBUG

MERRY OLD LAND OF OZ
EDELWEISS
DO-RE-MI

IT HAD TO BE YOU CD – IMPORT
IT HAD TO BE YOU
I COULD WRITE A BOOK
BUT NOT FOR ME
STOMPIN AT THE SAVOY
WHERE OR WHEN
IT'S ALRIGHT WITH ME
PROMISE ME YOU'LL REMEMBER
WE ARE IN LOVE
FOREVER FOR NOW
LOFTY'S ROACH SOUFFLE
DON'T GET AROUND MUCH ANYMORE
RECIPE FOR LOVE

**HARRY CONNICK JR. / IN CONCERT
ON BROADWAY
DVD /CD - 2 DISC SET
DISC 1**
WE ARE IN LOVE
THE WAY YOU LOOK TONIGHT
BÉSAME MUCHO
THE OTHER HOURS

NOWHERE WITH LOVE
HOW INSENSITIVE
COME BY ME
MY TIME OF DAY/I'VE NEVER BEEN IN
LOVE BEFORE
ALL THE WAY
BAYOU MAHARAJAH
RECIPE FOR LOVE
HEAR ME IN THE HARMONY
LIGHT THE WAY
TUG BOAT
ST. JAMES INFIRMARY BLUES
TAKE HER TO THE MARDI GRAS
HOW COME YOU DO ME LIKE YOU DO?
OH, DIDN'T HE RAMBLE
BOURBON STREET PARADE
MARDI GRAS IN NEW ORLEANS
A CONVERSATION WITH HARRY
DISC2
WE ARE IN LOVE
THE WAY YOU LOOK TONIGHT
BÉSAME MUCHO
THE OTHER HOURS
NOWHERE WITH LOVE
HOW INSENSITIVE
COME BY ME

MY TIME OF DAY/I'VE NEVER BEEN
IN LOVE BEFORE
ALL THE WAY
BAYOU MAHARAJAH
HEAR ME IN THE HARMONY
LIGHT THE WAY
TAKE HER TO THE MARDI GRAS
BOURBON STREET PARADE
MARDI GRAS IN NEW ORLEANS

**ONLY YOU CONCERT: IN CONCERT
[DVD & CD]**
SAVE THE LAST DANCE FOR ME [DVD]
FOR ONCE IN MY LIFE [DVD]
GOOD NIGHT MY LOVE (PLEASANT
DREAMS) [DVD]
IT MIGHT AS WELL BE SPRING [DVD]
WE ARE IN LOVE [DVD]
VERY THOUGHT OF YOU [DVD]
YOU DON'T KNOW ME [DVD]
BOURBON STREET PARADE [DVD]
THERE IS ALWAYS ONE MORE TIME
[DVD]
SWEET GEORGIA BROWN [DVD]
I STILL GET JEALOUS [DVD]
OTHER HOURS [DVD]

MY BLUE HEAVEN [DVD]
ONLY YOU (AND YOU ALONE) [DVD]
I'M WALKIN' [DVD]
COME BY ME [DVD]
SAVE THE LAST DANCE FOR ME
FOR ONCE IN MY LIFE
IT MIGHT AS WELL BE SPRING
VERY THOUGHT OF YOU
YOU DON'T KNOW ME
BOURBON STREET PARADE
THERE IS ALWAYS ONE MORE TIME
SWEET GEORGIA BROWN
I STILL GET JEALOUS
OTHER HOURS
MY BLUE HEAVEN
ONLY YOU (AND YOU ALONE)
I'M WALKIN'
COME BY ME

HARRY CONNICK JR. - NOW SEE HEAR (G): DVD
SWEET GEORGIA BROWN
DON'T GET AROUND MUCH ANY MORE
RECIPE FOR LOVE
BARE NECESSITIES
THEY CAN'T TAKE THAT AWAY FROM ME

YOU DIDN'T KNOW ME WHEN
HE IS, THEY ARE
WITH IMAGINATION
WE ARE IN LOVE
IT HAD TO BE YOU
JUST KISS ME
ALL OF ME
PARAMOUNT FANFARE

HARRY CONNICK JR DVD - THE NEW YORK BIG BAND CONCERT

INTRO - HARRY CONNICK JR
SWEET GEORGIA BROWN
DON'T GET AROUND MUCH ANYMORE
RECIPE FOR LOVE
BARE NECESSITIES
THEY CAN'T TAKE THAT AWAY FROM ME
YOU DIDN'T KNOW ME WHEN
HE IS, THEY ARE
WITH IMAGINATION
WE ARE IN LOVE
IT HAD TO BE YOU
JUST KISS ME
ALL OF ME
PARAMOUNT FANFARE
END CREDIT ROLL

BIBLIOGRAPHY

ELEVEN:
http://www.harryconnickjr.com/us/music/eleven

BLUE LIGHT, RED LIGHT:
http://www.harryconnickjr.com/us/music/blue-light-red-light

WE ARE IN LOVE:
http://www.harryconnickjr.com/us/music/we-are-love

LOFTY'S ROACH SOUFFLE:
http://www.harryconnickjr.com/us/music/loftys-roach-souffle

WHEN HARRY MET SALLY... MUSIC FROM THE MOTION PICTURE:
http://www.harryconnickjr.com/us/music/when-harry-met-sally-music-motion-picture

HARRY CONNICK JR DVD - THE NEW YORK BIG BAND CONCERT:
http://au.shopping.com/harry-connick-jr-dvd-/aVMO07roOkDXKSz5YuFoCQ==/info

20:
http://www.harryconnickjr.com/us/music/20

HARRY CONNICK, JR.:
http://www.harryconnickjr.com/us/music/harry-connick-jr

FRANCE I WISH YOU LOVE CD:
http://www.cduniverse.com/productinfo.asp?pid=1245362&cart=1155190067

COME BY ME/SONGS I HEARD CD:
http://www.cduniverse.com/productinfo.asp?pid=7760553

HARRY CONNICK JR. - NOW SEE HEAR (G): DVD:
http://www.dvdwarehouse.com.au/harry-connick-jr.-now-see-hear.html

HARRY CONNICK JR. / IN CONCERT ON BROADWAY -DVD /CD - 2 DISC SET:
http://www.blue-eyes.com/magento/harry-connick-jr-in-concert-on-broadway-dvd-cd-2-disc-set.html

IT HAD TO BE YOU CD – IMPORT:
http://www.cduniverse.com/productinfo.a
sp?pid=1267687

ONLY YOU CONCERT: IN CONCERT [DVD
& CD] BY HARRY CONNICK, JR:
http://new.music.yahoo.com/harry-
connick-jr/albums/only-you-concert-in-
concert-dvd-cd--194347021

TONY BENNETT

TONY BENNETT - SINGS RODGERS & HART SONGS CD
THIS CAN'T BE LOVE
THIS CAN'T BE LOVE
BLUE MOON
BLUE MOON
THE LADY IS A TRAMP
THE LADY IS A TRAMP
LOVER
LOVER
MANHATTAN
MANHATTAN
SPRING IS HERE
SPRING IS HERE
HAVE YOU MET MISS JONES?

HAVE YOU MET MISS JONES?
ISN'T IT ROMANTIC?
ISN'T IT ROMANTIC?
WAIT TILL YOU SEE HER
WAIT TILL YOU SEE HER
I COULD WRITE A BOOK
I COULD WRITE A BOOK
THOU SWELL
THOU SWELL
THE MOST BEAUTIFUL GIRL IN THE
WORLD
THE MOST BEAUTIFUL GIRL IN THE
WORLD
THERE'S A SMALL HOTEL
THERE'S A SMALL HOTEL
I'VE GOT FIVE DOLLARS
I'VE GOT FIVE DOLLARS
YOU TOOK ADVANTAGE OF ME
YOU TOOK ADVANTAGE OF ME
I WISH I WERE IN LOVE AGAIN
I WISH I WERE IN LOVE AGAIN
THIS FUNNY WORLD
THIS FUNNY WORLD
MY HEART STOOD STILL
MY HEART STOOD STILL
MY ROMANCE

MY ROMANCE
MOUNTAIN GREENERY
MOUNTAIN GREENERY
THIS CAN'T BE LOVE
THIS CAN'T BE LOVE
I COULD WRITE A BOOK
I COULD WRITE A BOOK
THOU SWELL
THOU SWELL
MOST BEAUTIFUL GIRL IN THE WORLD
MOST BEAUTIFUL GIRL IN THE WORLD
I WISH I WERE IN LOVE AGAIN
I WISH I WERE IN LOVE AGAIN
THIS FUNNY WORLD
THIS FUNNY WORLD

TONY BENNETT - GREATEST HITS OF THE '60S CD

PUT ON A HAPPY FACE
THE BEST IS YET TO COME
ONCE UPON A TIME
I LEFT MY HEART IN SAN FRANCISCO
I WANNA BE AROUND
THE GOOD LIFE
THIS IS ALL I ASK
WHEN JOANNA LOVED ME

SPEAK LOW
WHO CAN I TURN TO? (WHEN NOBODY
NEEDS ME)
IF I RULED THE WORLD
FLY ME TO THE MOON (IN OTHER
WORDS)
THE SHADOW OF YOUR SMILE
FOR ONCE IN MY LIFE
MY FAVORITE THINGS
SOMETHING

TONY BENNETT - CLOUD 7 CD
I FALL IN LOVE TOO EASILY
MY BABY JUST CARES FOR ME
MY HEART TELLS ME (SHOULD I
BELIEVE MY HEART?)
OLD DEVIL MOON
LOVE LETTERS
MY REVERIE
GIVE ME THE SIMPLE LIFE
WHILE THE MUSIC PLAYS ON
I CAN'T BELIEVE THAT YOU'RE IN LOVE
WITH ME
DARN THAT DREAM

TONY BENNETT - THE MOVIE SONG ALBUM CD

SONG FROM "THE OSCAR" (MAYBE SEPTEMBER)
GIRL TALK: - MONK MONTGOMERY
THE GENTLE RAIN
EMILY
THE PAWNBROKER
SAMBA DE ORFEU
THE SHADOW OF YOUR SMILE
SMILE
THE SECOND TIME AROUND
DAYS OF WINE AND ROSES
NEVER TOO LATE
THE TROLLEY SONG

TONY BENNETT - MTV UNPLUGGED CD

OLD DEVIL MOON
SPEAK LOW
IT HAD TO BE YOU
I LOVE A PIANO
IT AMAZES ME
YOU'RE ALL THE WORLD TO ME
RAGS TO RICHES
WHEN JOANNA LOVED ME

GIRL I LOVE, THE (A.K.A. THE MAN I LOVE)
FLY ME TO THE MOON (IN OTHER WORDS)
THE GOOD LIFE / I WANNA BE AROUND
I LEFT MY HEART IN SAN FRANCISCO
STEPPIN' OUT WITH MY BABY
MOONGLOW: - K.D. LANG
THEY CAN'T TAKE THAT AWAY FROM ME: - ELVIS COSTELLO, ELVIS COSTELLO
A FOGGY DAY
ALL OF YOU
BODY AND SOUL
IT DON'T MEAN A THING IF IT AIN'T GOT THAT SWING
AUTUMN LEAVES / INDIAN SUMMER
JUST A LITTLE STREET WHERE OLD FRIENDS MEET
WHEN DO THE BELLS FOR ME

TONY BENNETT SINGS HIS ALL-TIME HALL OF FAME HITS CD
BECAUSE OF YOU: - MONO
COLD, COLD HEART
RAGS TO RICHES: - MONO
ONE FOR MY BABY / IT HAD TO BE YOU

I LEFT MY HEART IN SAN FRANCISCO
I WANNA BE AROUND
THIS IS ALL I ASK
THE GOOD LIFE
THE SHADOW OF YOUR SMILE
WHO CAN I TURN TO (WHEN NOBODY
NEEDS ME)
YESTERDAY I HEARD THE RAIN
FOR ONCE IN MY LIFE

TONY BENNETT - SING THE ULTIMATE AMERICAN SONGBOOK VOL. 1 CD

ANYTHING GOES: - HIS ORCHESTRA
THE VERY THOUGHT OF YOU
THE WAY YOU LOOK TONIGHT
EV'RY TIME WE SAY GOODBYE
THAT OLD BLACK MAGIC
A FOGGY DAY
I'LL BE SEEING YOU
AIN'T MISBEHAVIN'
IT HAD TO BE YOU
MOONGLOW
SHE'S FUNNY THAT WAY
YOU GO TO MY HEAD
THEY CAN'T TAKE THAT AWAY FROM ME

YOU'LL NEVER GET AWAY FROM ME
TAKING A CHANCE OF LOVE

**TONY BENNETT - IF I RULED THE
WORLD: SONGS FOR
THE JET SET CD**
SAMBA DO AVIAO
FLY ME TO THE MOON
HOW INSENSITIVE
IF I RULED THE WORLD
LOVE SCENE
TAKE THE MOMENT
THEN WAS THEN AND NOW IS NOW
SWEET LORRAINE
THE RIGHT TO LOVE
WATCH WHAT HAPPENS
ALL MY TOMORROWS
TWO BY TWO
FALLING IN LOVE WITH LOVE

**TONY BENNETT - BEAT OF MY
HEART CD**
LET'S BEGIN
LULLABY OF BROADWAY
LET THERE BE LOVE
LOVE FOR SALE

CRAZY RHYTHM
BEAT OF MY HEART, THE: - CHICO
HAMILTON
SO BEATS MY HEART FOR YOU
BLUES IN THE NIGHT
LAZY AFTERNOON: - CHICO HAMILTON
LET'S FACE THE MUSIC AND DANCE
JUST ONE OF THOSE THINGS
IT'S SO PEACEFUL IN THE COUNTRY
IN SANDY'S EYES
I GET A KICK OUT OF YOU
YOU GO TO MY HEAD
I ONLY HAVE EYES FOR YOU
BEGIN THE BEGUINE

TONY BENNETT - I WANNA BE AROUND CD

THE GOOD LIFE
IF I LOVE AGAIN
I WANNA BE AROUND
I'VE GOT YOUR NUMBER
UNTIL I MET YOU
ONCE UPON A SUMMERTIME
IF YOU WERE MINE
I WILL LIVE MY LIFE FOR YOU
SOMEONE TO LOVE

IT WAS ME
QUIET NIGHTS OF QUIET STARS
(CORCOVADO)
IF I LOVE AGAIN
THE WAY THAT I FEEL
THE MOMENT OF TRUTH
GOT HER OFF MY HANDS (BUT CAN'T
GET HER OFF MY MIND)
'LONG ABOUT NOW
YOUNG AND FOOLISH
TRICKS

MY BEST TO YOU CD
THE SECOND TIME AROUN
I WANNA BE AROUND
I LEFT MY HEART IN SAN FRANCISCO
FOR ONCE IN MY LIFE
LOVE STORY, (WHERE DO I BEGIN)
A TASTE OF HONEY
WHO CAN I TURN TO (WHEN NOBODY
NEEDS ME)
IT HAD TO BE YOU
THE SHADOW OF YOUR SMILE
WHAT A WONDERFUL WORLD

TONY BENNETT - SOMETHING CD
SOMETHING
THE LONG AND WINDING ROAD
EVERYBODY'S TALKIN'
ON A CLEAR DAY (YOU CAN SEE
FOREVER)
COCO
THINK HOW IT'S GONNA BE
WAVE
MAKE IT EASY ON YOURSELF
COME SATURDAY MORNING
WHEN I LOOK IN YOUR EYES
YELLOW DAYS
WHAT A WONDERFUL WORLD

TONY BENNETT - HAVE I TOLD YOU LATELY CD
THIS IS ALL I ASK
THESE FOOLISH THINGS (REMIND ME
OF YOU)
HAVE I TOLD YOU LATELY?
ALL OF ME
TENDERLY
WHEN JOANNA LOVED ME
I GOT LOST IN HER ARMS
TIME AFTER TIME

ALWAYS
MAYBE THIS TIME

TONY BENNETT - I LEFT MY HEART IN SAN FRANCISCO CD

LEFT MY HEART IN SAN FRANCISCO
ONCE UPON A TIME
TENDER IS THE NIGHT
SMILE
LOVE FOR SALE
TAKING A CHANCE ON LOVE
CANDY KISSES
HAVE I TOLD YOU LATELY?
RULES OF THE ROAD
MARRY YOUNG
I'M ALWAYS CHASING RAINBOWS
THE BEST IS YET TO COME

TONY BENNETT - GREATEST HITS OF THE '50S CD

BOULEVARD OF BROKEN DREAMS, THE
(GIGOLO AND GIGOLETTE)
BECAUSE OF YOU
COLD, COLD HEART
BLUE VELVET
RAGS TO RICHES

STRANGER IN PARADISE
SING YOU SINNERS
JUST IN TIME
CA, C'EST L'AMOUR
IT AMAZES ME
FIREFLY
THE PARTY'S OVER
LOST IN THE STARS
LULLABY OF BROADWAY
SMILE
CLIMB EV'RY MOUNTAIN

TONY BENNETT - LIFE IS BEAUTIFUL CD

LIFE IS BEAUTIFUL
LIFE IS BEAUTIFUL
ALL MINE
ALL MINE
BRIDGES
BRIDGES
REFLECTIONS
REFLECTIONS
EXPERIMENT
EXPERIMENT
THIS FUNNY WORLD
THIS FUNNY WORLD

AS TIME GOES BY
AS TIME GOES BY
I USED TO BE COLOR BLIND
I USED TO BE COLOR BLIND
LOST IN THE STARS
LOST IN THE STARS
THERE'LL BE SOME CHANGES MADE
THERE'LL BE SOME CHANGES MADE
WHAT IS THIS THING CALLED LOVE /
LOVE FOR SALE / YOU'D BE SO NICE TO
COME HOME TO / EASY TO
LOVE / IT'S ALRIGHT WITH ME / NIGHT
AND DAY / DREAM DANCING / I'VE GOT
YOU UNDER MY SKIN
WHAT IS THIS THING CALLED LOVE /
LOVE FOR SALE / YOU'D BE SO NICE TO
COME HOME TO / EASY TO LOVE / IT'S
ALRIGHT WITH ME / NIGHT AND
DAY / DREAM DANCING / I'VE GOT YOU
UNDER MY SKIN

**TONY BENNETT - THIS IS JAZZ #33
CD**
DANCING IN THE DARK
WHEN LIGHTS ARE LOW
OUT OF THIS WORLD

LET'S FACE THE MUSIC AND DANCE
SOLITUDE
CRAZY RHYTHM
CLOSE YOUR EYES
JUDY
LOVE SCENE
HAVE YOU MET MISS JONES?
WHILE THE MUSIC PLAYS ON
JUST ONE OF THOSE THINGS
SWEET LORRAINE
DANNY BOY

YOUNG TONY BENNETT CD
JUST SAY I LOVE HER
OUR LADY OF FATIMA
ONE LIE LEADS TO ANOTHER
DON'T CRY, BABY
BEAUTIFUL MADNESS
THE VALENTINO TANGO
WHILE WE'RE YOUNG
COLD, COLD HEART
PLEASE, MY LOVE
SILLY DREAMER
SINCE MY LOVE HAS GONE
SOMEWHERE ALONG THE WAY
SLEEPLESS

HAVE A GOOD TIME
ROSES OF YESTERDAY
I'M LOST AGAIN
YOU COULD MAKE ME SMILE AGAIN
CONGRATULATIONS TO SOMEONE
NO ONE WILL EVER KNOW
I'M THE KING OF BROKEN HEARTS
SOMEONE TURNED THE MOON UPSIDE
DOWN
I'LL GO
RAGS TO RICHES
HERE COMES THAT HEARTACHE AGAIN
STRANGER IN PARADISE
WHY DOES IT HAVE TO BE ME?

TONY BENNETT - GOOD LIFE CD
I LEFT MY HEART IN SAN FRANCISCO
ONCE UPON A TIME
YOUNG AND WARM AND WONDERFUL
COME RAIN OR COME SHINE
YOU'LL NEVER GET AWAY FROM ME
THE GOOD LIFE
THIS IS ALL I ASK
TAKING A CHANCE ON LOVE
FLY ME TO THE MOON
MY FUNNY VALENTINE

ESSENCE OF TONY BENNETT CD
BECAUSE OF YOU
SOLITAIRE
LAZY AFTERNOON
I LEFT MY HEART IN SAN FRANCISCO
IF LOVE AGAIN
WHEN JOANNA LOVED ME
SOMETHING IN YOUR SMILE
YESTERDAY I HEARD THE RAIN
ALL MY TOMORROWS
WAVE

TONY BENNETT - BENNETT/BERLIN CD
THEY SAY IT'S WONDERFUL
ISN'T THIS A LOVELY DAY?
ALL OF MY LIFE: - (WITH DEXTER
GORDON, DEXTER GORDON)
NOW IT CAN BE TOLD
THE SONG IS ENDED
WHEN I LOST YOU
CHEEK TO CHEEK: - (WITH GEORGE
BENSON, GEORGE BENSON)
LET YOURSELF GO
LET'S FACE THE MUSIC AND DANCE
SHAKING THE BLUES AWAY

RUSSIAN LULLABY: - (WITH DIZZY GILLESPIE)
WHITE CHRISTMAS: - DEXTER GORDON, TONY BENNETT / DEXTER GORDON

ARTIST'S CHOICE: TONY BENNETT
CD

TENDERLY
APRIL IN PARIS
I LOVE SAMANTHA
OVER THE RAINBOW
TEA FOR TWO
SEPTEMBER SONG
SENTIMENTAL JOURNEY
THEME FROM THE THREEPENNY OPERA, A (MACK THE KNIFE)
STRAIGHTEN UP AND FLY RIGHT
RAVEL, STRING QUARTET IN F MAJOR, II ASSEZ, TRES RYTHME
TAKE THE "A" TRAIN
ONE FOR MY BABY (AND ONE MORE FOR THE ROAD)
I WISHED ON THE MOON
TOO DARN HOT
BY MYSELF
I WANT TO RIDE THAT GLORY TRAIN

TONY BENNETT - CLASSIC COLLECTION CD

DISC 1

I FALL IN LOVE TOO EASILY
MY BABY JUST CARES FOR ME
MY HEART TELLS ME (SHOULD I
BELIEVE MY HEART?)
OLD DEVIL MOON
LOVE LETTERS
MY REVERIE
GIVE ME THE SIMPLE LIFE
WHILE THE MUSIC PLAYS ON
I CAN'T BELIEVE THAT YOU'RE IN LOVE
WITH ME
DARN THAT DREAM

DISC 2

LET'S BEGIN
LULLABY OF BROADWAY
LET THERE BE LOVE
LOVE FOR SALE
CRAZY RHYTHM: - CHICO HAMILTON
BEAT OF MY HEART, THE
SO BEATS MY HEART FOR YOU
BLUES IN THE NIGHT
LAZY AFTERNOON
LET'S FACE THE MUSIC AND DANCE

189

JUST ONE OF THOSE THINGS
IT'S SO PEACEFUL IN THE COUNTRY
IN SANDY'S EYES: - CHICO HAMILTON
I GET A KICK OUT OF YOU
YOU GO TO MY HEAD
I ONLY HAVE EYES FOR YOU
BEGIN THE BEGUINE

DISC 3

I DIDN'T KNOW WHAT TIME IT WAS
BEWITCHED
NOBODY'S HEART BELONGS TO ME
I'M THROUGH WITH LOVE
MY FUNNY VALENTINE
THE MAN THAT GOT AWAY
WHERE OR WHEN
A SLEEPIN' BEE
HAPPINESS IS A THING CALLED JOE
MAM'SELLE
JUST FRIENDS
STREET OF DREAMS

DISC 4

I LEFT MY HEART IN SAN FRANCISCO
ONCE UPON A TIME
TENDER IS THE NIGHT
SMILE
LOVE FOR SALE: - BILLY EXINER

TAKING A CHANCE ON LOVE: - COUNT
BASIE & HIS ORCHESTRA
CANDY KISSES
HAVE I TOLD YOU LATELY?
RULES OF THE ROAD
MARRY YOUNG
I'M ALWAYS CHASING RAINBOWS

TONY BENNETT - STEPPIN' OUT CD
STEPPIN' OUT WITH MY BABY
WHO CARES?
TOP HAT, WHITE TIE AND TAILS
THEY CAN'T TAKE THAT AWAY FROM ME
DANCING IN THE DARK
SHINE ON YOUR SHOES
HE LOVES AND SHE LOVES
THEY ALL LAUGHED
I CONCENTRATE ON YOU
YOU'RE ALL THE WORLD TO ME
ALL OF YOU
NICE WORK IF YOU CAN GET IT
IT ONLY HAPPENS WHEN I DANCE WITH
YOU
SHALL WE DANCE
YOU'RE EASY TO DANCE WITH /
CHANGE PARTNERS / CHEEK TO CHEEK

I GUESS I'LL HAVE TO CHANGE MY PLAN
THAT'S ENTERTAINMENT
BY MYSELF

**TONY BENNETT - COLLECTION: I
LEFT MY HEART IN SAN
FRANCISCO/ART OF
EXCELLENCE/ASTORIA CD
DISC 1**
IN SAN FRANCISCO (I LEFT MY HEART)
ONCE UPON A TIME
TENDER IS THE NIGHT
SMILE
LOVE FOR SALE
TAKING A CHANCE ON LOVE
CANDY KISSES
HAVE I TOLD YOU LATELY?
RULES OF THE ROAD
MARRY YOUNG
I'M ALWAYS CHASING RAINBOWS
THE BEST IS YET TO COME SEE ALL
DISC 2
WHY DO PEOPLE FALL IN LOVE
MOMENTS LIKE THIS
WHAT ARE YOU AFRAID OF?
WHEN LOVE WAS ALL WE HAD

SO MANY STARS
EVERYBODY HAS THE BLUES
CITY OF THE ANGELS
HOW DO YOU KEEP THE MUSIC
PLAYING?
FORGET THE WOMAN
A RAINY DAY
I GOT LOST IN HER ARMS
THE DAY YOU LEAVE ME

DISC 3

WHEN DO THE BELLS RING FOR ME
I WAS LOST, I WAS DRIFTING
A LITTLE STREET WHERE OLD FRIENDS
MEET
THE GIRL I LOVE
IT'S LIKE REACHING FOR THE MOON
SPEAK LOW
THE FOLKS WHO LIVE ON THE HILL
ANTONIA
A WEAVER OF DREAMS / THERE WILL
NEVER BE ANOTHER YOU
BODY AND SOUL
WHERE DO YOU GO FROM LOVE
THE BOULEVARD OF BROKEN DREAMS
WHERE DID THE MAGIC GO
I'VE COME HOME AGAIN

TONY BENNETT - JAZZ CD

I CAN'T BELIEVE THAT YOU'RE IN LOVE
WITH ME
DON'T GET AROUND MUCH ANYMORE
STELLA BY STARLIGHT
ON GREEN DOLPHIN STREET
LET'S FACE THE MUSIC AND DANCE
I'M THRU WITH LOVE
SOLITUDE
LULLABY OF BROADWAY
DANCING IN THE DARK
I LET A SONG GO OUT OF MY HEART
WHEN LIGHTS ARE LOW
JUST ONE OF THOSE THINGS
CRAZY RHYTHM
STREET OF DREAMS
LOVE SCENE
WHILE THE MUSIC PLAYS ON
CLOSE YOUR EYES
CLEAR OUT OF THIS WORLD
JUST FRIENDS
HAVE YOU MET MISS JONES?
DANNY BOY
SWEET LORRAINE

TONY BENNETT - JAZZ MOODS: COOL CD
LET'S BEGIN
LOVE SCENE
CARAVAN
SWEET LORRAINE
CLOSE YOUR EYES
UNTIL I MET YOU
I GET A KICK OUT OF YOU
STELLA BY STARLIGHT
DANCING IN THE DARK
THAT OLD BLACK MAGIC
CRAZY RHYTHM
WRAP YOUR TROUBLES IN DREAMS
(AND DREAM YOUR TROUBLES AWAY)
OUT OF THIS WORLD
IT DON'T MEAN A THING (IF IT AIN'T
GOT THAT SWING)

PLAYLIST: THE VERY BEST OF TONY BENNETT CD
PUT ON A HAPPY FACE
I LEFT MY HEART IN SANFRANCISCO
UNTIL I MET YOU
I WANNA BE AROUND
WHEN JOANNA LOVED ME

WHO CAN I TURN TO (WHEN NOBODY
NEEDS ME)
HAVE YOU MET MISS JONES?
THE SHADOW OF YOUR SMILE
THE GENTLE RAIN
SONG FROM "THE OSCAR" (MAYBE
SEPTEMBER)
FOR ONCE IN MY LIFE
HOW DO YOU KEEP THE MUSIC PLAYING
MOOD INDIGO
STEPPIN' OUT WITH MY BABY

TONY BENNETT - MOVIE SONG ALBUM CD

SONG FROM "THE OSCAR" (MAYBE
SEPTEMBER)
GIRL TALK
THE GENTLE RAIN
EMILY
THE PAWNBROKER
SAMBA DE ORFEU
THE SHADOW OF YOUR SMILE
SMILE
THE SECOND TIME AROUND
DAYS OF WINE AND ROSES
NEVER TOO LATE

THE TROLLEY SONG

TONY BENNETT - ASTORIA: PORTRAIT OF THE ARTIST CD
WHEN DO THE BELLS RING FOR ME
I WAS LOST, I WAS DRIFTING
A LITTLE STREET WHERE OLD FRIENDS MEET
THE GIRL I LOVE
IT'S LIKE REACHING FOR THE MOON
SPEAK LOW
THE FOLKS THAT LIVE ON THE HILL
ANTONIA
A WEAVER OF DREAMS / THERE WILL NEVER BE ANOTHER YOU
BODY AND SOUL
WHERE DO YOU GO FROM LOVE
THE BOULEVARD OF BROKEN DREAMS
WHERE DID THE MAGIC GO
I'VE COME HOME AGAIN

TONY BENNETT - FOR ONCE IN MY LIFE/I'VE GOTTA BE ME CD
THEY CAN'T TAKE THAT AWAY FROM ME: - BURT COLLINS
SOMETHING IN YOUR SMILE

DAYS OF LOVE (THEME FROM "HOMBRE")

BROADWAY/CRAZY RHYTHM/LULLABY OF BROADWAY

FOR ONCE IN MY LIFE

SOMETIMES I'M HAPPY

OUT OF THIS WORLD

BABY, DREAM YOUR DREAM

HOW DO YOU SAY AUF WIEDERSEHEN

I'VE GOTTA BE ME

KEEP SMILING AT TROUBLE (TROUBLE'S A BUBBLE)

OVER THE SUN

BURT COLLINS

PLAY IT AGAIN, SAM: - BURT COLLINS, MARKY MARKOWITZ

ALFIE

WHAT THE WORLD NEEDS NOW IS LOVE

BABY DON'T YOU QUIT NOW

THAT NIGHT

THEY ALL LAUGHED

A LONELY PLACE

WHOEVER YOU ARE, I LOVE YOU

THEME FROM "VALLEY OF THE DOLLS"

TONY BENNETT - HAVE YOU MET MISS JONES? CD

HAVE YOU MET MISS JONES?
THIS CAN'T BE LOVE
BLUE MOON
THE LADY IS A TRAMP
MANHATTAN
ISN'T IT ROMANTIC
THERE'S A SMALL HOTEL
MY ROMANCE
THERE'LL BE SOME CHANGES MADE
AS TIME GOES BY

TONY BENNETT - BLUE VELVET CD

BLUE VELVET
I WON'T CRY ANYMORE
SILLY DREAMER
SOMEWHERE ALONG THE WAY
ONCE THERE LIVED A FOOL
BECAUSE OF YOU
THE VALENTINO TANGO
SLEEPLESS
I CAN'T GIVE YOU ANYTHING BUT LOVE
COLD, COLD HEART
THE BOULEVARD OF BROKEN DREAMS
WHILE WE'RE YOUNG

I WANNA BE LOVED
STAY WHERE YOU ARE
CONGRATULATIONS TO SOMEONE
SINCE MY LOVE HAS GONE
RAGS TO RICHES
TAKE ME
HERE COMES THAT HEARTACHE AGAIN
STRANGER IN PARADISE

TONY BENNETT - PERFECTLY FRANK CD

TIME AFTER TIME
I FALL IN LOVE TOO EASILY
EAST OF THE SUN (WEST OF THE
MOON)
NANCY
I THOUGHT ABOUT YOU
NIGHT AND DAY
I'VE GOT THE WORLD ON A STRING
I'M GLAD THERE IS YOU
A NIGHTINGALE SANG IN BERKELEY
SQUARE
I WISHED ON THE MOON
YOU GO TO MY HEAD
THE LADY IS A TRAMP
I SEE YOUR FACE BEFORE ME

DAY IN, DAY OUT
INDIAN SUMMER
CALL ME IRRESPONSIBLE
HERE'S THAT RAINY DAY
LAST NIGHT WHEN WE WERE YOUNG
I WISH I WERE IN LOVE AGAIN
A FOGGY DAY
DON'T WORRY 'BOUT ME
ONE FOR MY BABY
ANGEL EYES
I'LL BE SEEING YOU

TONY BENNETT - VERY THOUGHT OF YOU CD

JUST IN TIME
DON'T GET AROUND MUCH ANYMORE
THE VERY THOUGHT OF YOU
STRANGER IN PARADISE
THE SECOND TIME AROUND
STELLA BY STARLIGHT
IT'S MAGIC
LAURA
IF I LOVE AGAIN
I'LL BE AROUND

TONY BENNETT - WHO CAN I TURN TO CD

WHO CAN I TURN TO (WHEN NOBODY NEEDS ME)
WRAP YOUR TROUBLES IN DREAMS (AND DREAM YOUR TROUBLES AWAY)
THERE'S A LULL IN MY LIFE
AUTUMN LEAVES
I WALK A LITTLE FASTER
THE BRIGHTEST SMILE IN TOWN
I'VE NEVER SEEN
BETWEEN THE DEVIL AND THE DEEP BLUE SEA
LISTEN, LITTLE GIRL
GOT THE GATE ON THE GOLDEN GATE
WALTZ FOR DEBBY
THE BEST THING IS TO BE A PERSON

TONY BENNETT - SINGIN' AND SWINGIN' CD

MAKIN' WHOOPEE
NIGHT AND DAY
IN THE MIDDLE OF AN ISLAND
THOU SWELL

TONY BENNETT - I LEFT MY HEART IN SAN FRANCISCO/PERFECTLY FRANK CD

DISC 1

I LEFT MY HEART IN SAN FRANCISCO

ONCE UPON A TIME (FROM ALL AMERICAN)

TENDER IS THE NIGHT (FROM TENDER IS THE NIGHT)

SMILE (FROM MODERN TIMES)

LOVE FOR SALE (FROM THE NEW YORKERS): - BILLY EXINER

TAKING A CHANCE ON LOVE (FROM CABIN IN THE SKY)

CANDY KISSES

HAVE I TOLD YOU LATELY (FROM I CAN GET IT FOR YOU WHOLESALE)

RULES OF THE ROAD

MARRY YOUNG

I'M ALWAYS CHASING RAINBOWS (FROM OH, LOOK!)

THE BEST IS YET TO COME

DISC 2

TIME AFTER TIME

I FALL IN LOVE TOO EASILY

EAST OF THE SUN (WEST OF THE MOON)
NANCY
I THOUGHT ABOUT YOU
NIGHT AND DAY
I'VE GOT THE WORLD ON A STRING
I'M GLAD THERE IS YOU
A NIGHTINGALE SANG IN BERKELEY SQUARE
I WISHED ON THE MOON
YOU GO TO MY HEAD
THE LADY IS A TRAMP
I SEE YOUR FACE BEFORE ME
DAY IN, DAY OUT
INDIAN SUMMER
CALL ME IRRESPONSIBLE (FROM PAPA'S DELICATE CONDITION)
HERE'S THAT RAINY DAY
LAST NIGHT WHEN WE WERE YOUNG
I WISH I WERE IN LOVE AGAIN
DON'T WORRY 'BOUT ME
A FOGGY DAY (FROM A DAMSEL IN DISTRESS)
ONE FOR MY BABY (AND ONE MORE FOR THE ROAD)
ANGEL EYES

I'LL BE SEEING YOU

TONY BENNETT - STRANGER IN PARADISE CD

STRANGER IN PARADISE
I CAN'T GIVE YOU ANYTHING BUT LOVE
NO ONE WILL EVER KNOW
BECAUSE OF YOU
WHILE WE'RE YOUNG
I'M THE KING OF THE BROKEN HEARTS
HERE COMES THAT HERTACHE AGAIN
DON'T CRY BABY
BEAUTIFUL MADNESS
SINCE MY LOVE HAS GONE
SOMEONE TURNED THE MOON UPSIDE
DOWN
YOU COULD MAKE ME SMILE AGAIN
TAKE ME
SOMEWHERE ALONG THE WAY
I'M LOST AGAIN
I WANNA BE LOVED

TONY BENNETT - RAGS TO RICHES: 23 EARLY HITS AND FAVORITES CD

COLD, COLD HEART
THE BOULEVARD OF BROKEN DREAMS

RAGS TO RICHES
BLUE VELVET
BECAUSE OF YOU
I WON'T CRY ANYMORE
STRANGER IN PARADISE
THE VALENTINO TANGO
SINCE MY LOVE HAS GONE
TAKE ME
I'M THE KING OF BROKEN HEARTS
NO ONE WILL EVER KNOW
ANYWHERE I WANDER
SOLITAIRE
HAVE A GOOD TIME
STAY WHERE YOU ARE
SING YOU SINNERS
ROSES OF YESTERDAY
HERE IN MY HEART
JUST SAY I LOVER HER
CONGRATULATIONS TO SOMEONE
PLEASE MY LOVE
OUR LADY OF FATIMA

TONY BENNETT - PLATINUM ANTHOLOGY CD
I GUESS I'LL HAVE TO CHANGE MY PLANS

WITH PLENTY OF MONEY AND YOU
CHICAGO
ANYTHING GOES
I'VE GROWN ACCUSTOMED TO HER
FACE
JEEPERS CREEPERS
POOR LITTLE RICH GIRL
ARE YOU HAVIN' ANY FUN
LIFE IS A SONG
GROWING PAINS
LIFE IS BEAUTIFUL
EXPERIMENT
AS TIME GOES BY
THERE'LL BE SOME CHANGES MADE
I LEFT MY HEART IN SAN FRANCISCO

**TONY BENNETT - BENNETT SINGS
ELLINGTON: HOT & COOL CD**
DO NOTHIN' TILL YOU HEAR FROM ME
MOON INDIGO
SHE'S GOT IT BAD (AND THAT AIN'T
GOOD)
CARAVAN
CHELSEA BRIDGE
AZURE
I'M JUST A LUCKY SO AND SO

IN A SENTIMENTAL MOOD
DON'T GET AROUND MUCH ANYMORE
SOPHISTICATED LADY
IN A MELLOW TONE
DAY DREAM
PRELUDE TO A KISS
IT DON'T MEAN A THING (IF IT AIN'T
GOT THAT SWING)

TONY BENNETT - ART OF ROMANCE CD

CLOSE ENOUGH FOR LOVE
ALL IN FUN
WHERE DO YOU START
LITTLE DID I DREAM
I REMEMBER YOU
TIME TO SMILE
ALL FOR YOU
THE BEST MAN
DON'T LIKE GOODBYES
BEING ALIVE
GONE WITH THE WIND

TONY BENNETT - COLLECTIONS CD

BECAUSE OF YOU
COLD, COLD HEART

RAGS TO RICHES
ONE FOR MY BABY/IT HAD TO BE YOU
I LEFT MY HEART IN SAN FRANCISCO
I WANNA BE AROUND
THIS IS ALL I ASK
THE GOOD LIFE
THE SHADOW OF YOUR SMILE
WHO CAN I TURN TO (WHEN NOBODY
NEEDS ME)
YESTERDAY I HEARD THE RAIN
FOR ONCE IN MY LIFE

ONLY THE BEST OF TONY BENNETT
CD
DISC 1
I LEFT MY HEART IN SAN FRANCISCO
ONCE UPON A TIME
YOUNG AND WARM AND WONDERFUL
COME RAIN OR COME SHINE
YOU'LL NEVER GET AWAY FROM ME
THE GOOD LIFE
THIS IS ALL I ASK
TAKING A CHANCE ON LOVE
FLY ME TO THE MOON (IN OTHER
WORDS)
MY FUNNY VALENTINE

DISC 2

JUST IN TIME
DON'T GET AROUND MUCH ANYMORE
THE VERY THOUGHT OF YOU
STRANGER IN PARADISE
THE SECOND TIME AROUND
STELLA BY STARLIGHT
IT'S MAGIC
LAURA
IF I LOVE AGAIN
I'LL BE AROUND

DISC 3

WHO CAN I TURN TO (WHEN NOBODY
NEEDS ME)
WRAP YOUR TROUBLES IN DREAMS
(AND DREAM YOUR TROUBLES AWAY)
THERE'S A LULL IN MY LIFE
AUTUMN LEAVES
I WALK A LITTLE FASTER
THE BRIGHTEST SMILE IN TOWN
I'VE NEVER SEEN
BETWEEN THE DEVIL AND THE DEEP
BLUE SEA
LISTEN, LITTLE GIRL
GOT THE GATE ON THE GOLDEN GATE
WALTZ FOR DEBBY

THE BEST THING TO BE IS A PERSON
DISC 4
THE SECOND TIME AROUND
I WANNA BE AROUND
I LEFT MY HEART IN SAN FRANCISCO
FOR ONCE IN MY LIFE
(WHERE DO I BEGIN) LOVE STORY
BECAUSE OF YOU
JUST ONE OF THOSE THINGS
WHO CAN I TURN TO (WHEN NOBODY
NEEDS ME)
IT HAD TO BE YOU
THE SHADOW OF YOUR SMILE

TONY BENNETT - PLAYIN' WITH MY FRIENDS: BENNETT SINGS THE BLUES CD

ALRIGHT, OKAY, YOU WIN
EVERYDAY (I HAVE THE BLUES)
DON'T CRY BABY
GOOD MORNING, HEARTACHE
LET THE GOOD TIMES ROLL
EVENIN'
I GOTTA RIGHT TO SING THE BLUES
KEEP THE FAITH, BABY
BLUE AND SENTIMENTAL

OLD COUNT BASIE IS GONE (OLD PINEY BROWN IS GONE)
NEW YORK STATE OF MIND
UNDECIDED BLUES
BLUES IN THE NIGHT
STORMY WEATHER
PLAYIN' WITH MY FRIENDS

TONY BENNETT - YOUNG TONY CD - IMPORT
BOULEVARD OF BROKEN DREAMS
I WANNA BE LOVED
I CANT GIVE YOU ANYTHING BUT LOVE
OUR LADY OF FATIMA
JUST SAY I LOVE HER
SING YOU SINNERS
KISS YOU
ONE LIE LEADS TO ANOTHER
DON'T CRY BABY
ONCE THERE LIVED A FOOL
BEAUTIFUL MADNESS
VALENTINO TANGO
I WON'T CRY ANYMORE
BECAUSE OF YOU
WHILE WE'RE YOUNG
COLD, COLD, HEART

SINCE MY LOVE HAS GONE
PLEASE, MY LOVE
BLUE VELVET
SOLITAIRE
SILLY DREAMER
SLEEPLESS
SOMEWHERE ALONG THE WAY
I'M LOST AGAIN
HAVE A GOOD TIME
HERE IN MY HEART
ROSES OF YESTERDAY
YOU COULD MAKE THE SMILE AGAIN
CONGRATULATIONS TO SOMEONE
ANYWHERE I WANDER
STAYWHERE YOU ARE
TAKE ME
NO ONE WILL EVER KNOW
(I'M) THE KING OF BROKEN HEARTS
I'LL GO
RAGS TO RICHES
HERE COMES THAT HEARTACHE AGAIN
SOMEONE TURNED THE MOON UPSIDE
DOWN
STRANGER IN PARADISE
WHY DOES IT HAVE TO BE ME
UNTIL YESTERDAY (NON E LA PIOGGIA)

PLEASE DRIVER (ONCE AROUND THE PARK AGAIN)
THERE'LL BE NO TEARDROPS TONIGHT
MY HEART WON'T SAY GOODBYE
TAKE ME BACK AGAIN
MADONNA, MADONNA
NOT AS A STRANGER
CINNAMON SINNER
OLD DEVIL MOON
FALL IN LOVE TOO EASILY

TONY BENNETT - BEST SINGER IN THE BUSINESS CD - IMPORT DISC 1
COLD, COLD HEART
THE BOULEVARD OF BROKEN DREAMS
BECAUSE OF YOU
I WON'T CRY ANYMORE
I'M THE KING OF BROKEN HEARTS
NO ONE WILL EVER KNOW
ANYWHERE I WANDER
SOLITAIRE
I WANNA BE LOVED
STAY WHERE YOU ARE
PLEASE DRIVER (ONCE AROUND THE PARK AGAIN)

UNTIL YESTERDAY (NON E LA PIOGGIA)
ONCE THERE LIVED A FOOL
SLEEPLESS
DISC 2
RAGS TO RICHES
BLUE VELVET
THERE'LL BE NO TEARDROPS TONIGHT
MY HEART WON'T SAY GOODBYE
SING YOU SINNERS
ROSES OF YESTERDAY
HERE IN MY HEART
CONGRATULATIONS TO SOMEONE
MADONNA, MADONNA
KISS YOU
CINAMON SINNER
TAKE ME BACK AGAIN
SILLY DREAMER
SOMEWHERE ALONG THE WAY
DISC 3
STRANGER IN PARADISE
WHY DOES IT HAVE TO BE ME
NOT AS A STRANGER
I CAN'T GIVE YOU ANYTHING BUT LOVE
WHILE WE'RE YOUNG
HAVE A GOOD TIME
HERE COMES THAT HEARTACHE AGAIN

YOU COULD MAKE ME SMILE AGAIN
FUNNY THING
MY PRETTY SHOO-GAH
I'M LOST AGAIN
BEAUTIFUL MADNESS
THE VALENTION TANGO
TAKE ME

TONY BENNETT - 16 MOST REQUESTED SONGS CD - IMPORT

BECAUSE OF YOU
STRANGER IN PARADISE
RAGS TO RICHES
BOULEVARD OF BROKEN DREAMS
COLD, COLD HEART
JUST IN TIME
I LEFT MY HEART IN SAN FRANCISCO
I WANNA BE AROUND
WHO CAN I TURN TO (WHEN NOBODY
NEEDS ME)
FOR ONCE IN MY LIFE
THIS IS ALL I ASK
SMILE SEE
TENDER IS THE NIGHT
SHADOW OF YOUR SMILE
(WHERE DO I BEGIN) LOVE STORY

TONY BENNETT - CLASSIC BENNETT: JAZZ SIDES CD - IMPORT

I FALL IN LOVE TOO EASILY
MY BABY JUST CARES FOR ME
MY HEART TELLS ME
OLD EVIL MOON
LOVE LETTERS
MY REVERIE
GIVE ME THE SIMPLE LIFE
WHILE THE MUSIC PLAYS ON
I CAN'T BELIEVE THAT YOU'RE IN LOVE
WITH ME
DARN THAT DREAM
LET'S BEGIN
LULLABY OF BROADWAY
LET THERE BE LOVE
LOVE FOR SALE
CRAZY RHYTHM
THE BEAT OF MY HEART
SO BEATS MY HEART FOR YOU
BLUES IN THE NIGHT
LAZY AFTERNOON
LET'S FACE THE MUSIC AND DANCE
JUST ONE OF THOSE THINGS

ARMY AIR CORPS SONG
RAG THE RICHES
CA, C'EST L'AMOUR
JUST IN TIME
SING YOU SINNERS

IN CONCERT CD - IMPORT
INTRO
THERE'LL BE SOME CHANGES MADE
THIS CAN'T BE LOVE
SING YOU SINNERS
O SOLE MIO
IT DON'T MEAN A THING (IF IT AIN'T
GOT THAT SWING)
SOLITUDE
I LEFT MY HEART IN SAN FRANCISCO
LULLABY OF BROADWAY
WHO CAN I TURN TO (WHEN NOBODY
NEEDS ME)
BECAUSE OF YOU
DON'T GET AROUND MUCH ANYMORE
JUST IN TIME
SOMETHING
SOPHISTICATED LADY
RAGS TO RICHES
MY FUNNY VALENTINE

FOR ONCE IN MY LIFE
CLOSING THEME (I LEFT MY HEART IN
SAN FRANCISCO)

TONY BENNETT - CLASSIC ALBUM COLLECTION CD - IMPORT
MIDNIGHT RABBIT
BISCO
CAPTAIN SHAKER
LOOKLOOKLOOK
DISCO SENSATION
ROCKET CITY
MOVE THE CROWED
SLOW INTERLUDE
BACK TO DEATH
MY TEACHER IS A ZOMBIE
BARBIE'S BACK BLOW VERSION
VOODOO CHILD
RADIO
I CAN'T STOP
BISCO MUSHROOM VERSION

TONY BENNETT - WHILE WE'RE YOUNG CD - IMPORT
I WON'T CRY ANYMORE
SILLY DREAMER

SOMEWHERE ALONG THE WAY
ONCE THERE LIVED A FOOL
BECAUSE OF YOU
SLEEPLESS
I CAN'T GIVE YOU ANYTHING BUT LOVE
WHILE WE'RE YOUNG
I WANNA BE LOVED
STAY WHERE YOU ARE
CONGRATULATIONS TO SOMEONE
HERE COMES THAT HEARTACHE AGAIN
YOU COULD MAKE ME SMILE AGAIN
I'M LOST AGAIN
BEAUTIFUL MADNESS
HAVE A GOOD TIME
KISS YOU
LIFE IS A SONG
WITH PLENTY OF MONEY AND YOU
JEEPERS CREEPERS
ANYTHING GOES
I'VE GROWN ACCUSTOMED TO HER
FACE

TONY BENNETT CD - IMPORT
FALL IN LOVE TOO EASILY
MY BABY JUST CARES FOR ME
OLD DEVIL MOON

MY HEART TELLS ME (SHOULD I
BELIEVE)
LOVE LETTERS
MY REVERIE
GIVE ME THE SIMPLE LIFE
WHILE THE MUSIC PLAYS ON
I CAN'T BELIEVE THAT YOU'RE IN
DARN THAT DREAM
IT HAD TO BE YOU
YOU CAN DEPEND ON ME
I'M JUST A LUCKY SO AND SO
TAKING A CHANCE ON LOVE
THESE FOOLISH THINGS
I CAN'T GIVE YOU ANYTHING BUT LOVE
BOULEVARD OF BROKEN DREAMS
I'LL BE SEEING YOU

TONY BENNETT - SONGS FROM THE HEART CD - IMPORT

COLE PORTER MEDLEY (NOT USED IN
STORY)
THE LADY IS A TRAMP
THERES A SMALL HOTEL
BLUE MOON
LUCKY TO BE ME
YOU DONT KNOW WHAT LOVE IS

MOUNTAIN GREENERY
MAKE SOMEONE HAPPY
LONELY GIRL
MANHATTAN
THOU SWELL
AS TIME GOES BY
LOVER
I WISH I WERE IN LOVE AGAIN
MY HEART STOOD STILL
THIS CANT BE LOVE
THE MOST BEAUTIFUL GIRL IN THE
WORLD
LONELY GIRL
MANHATTAN
THOU SWELL
AS TIME GOES BY
LOVER
I WISH I WERE IN LOVE AGAIN
MY HEART STOOD STILL
THIS CAN'T BE LOVE
MOST BEAUTIFUL GIRL IN THE WORLD

**TONY BENNETT - CHICAGO CD -
IMPORT**
WITH PLENTY OF MONEY AND YOU
GROWING PAINS

I GUESS I'LL HAVE TO CHANGE MY
PLANS
LIFE IS A SONG
ANYTHING GOES
ARE YOU HAVIN' ANY FUN?
JEEPERS CREEPERS
POOR LITTLE RICH GIRL
CHICAGO (THAT TODDLING TOWN)
I'VE GROWN ACCUSTOMED TO HER
FACE

**TONY BENNETT - LET THERE BE
LOVE CD - IMPORT**
LULLABY OF BROADWAY
LET THERE BE LOVE
LOVE FOR SALE
CRAZY RHYTHM
THE BEAT OF MY HEART
BLUES IN THE NIGHT
LAZY AFTERNOON
LET'S FACE THE MUSIC AND DANCE
JUST ONE OF THOSE THINGS
STRANGER IN PARADISE
RAGS TO RICHES
CLOSE YOUR EYES

TONY BENNETT - LIFE IS A SONG CD - IMPORT

I'LL GUESS ILL HAVE TO CHANGE MY PLANS
CHIGACO
WITH PLENT ON MONEY AND YOU
ANYTHING GOES
LIFE IS A SONG
IVE GROWN ACCUSTOMED TO HER FACE
JEEPER CREEPERS
OUT OF THE WINDOW
GROWING PAINS
BROADWAY
POOR LITTLE RICH GIRL
LESTER LEAPS IN
ARE YOU HAVIN ANY FUN
APRIL IN PARIS

TONY BENNETT - ORIGINALS CD - IMPORT

AS TIME GOES
BLUE MOON
THIS FUNNY WORLD EXPERIMENT
EXPERIMENT
MY ROMANCE
I COULD WRITE A BOOK

SPRING IS HERE
MANHATTAN
I'VE GOT FIVE DOLLARS
HAVE YOU MET MISS JONES?
CHICAGO

TONY BENNETT - PURELY CD - IMPORT

SOLITAIRE
TAKE ME BACK AGAIN
THERE'LL BE NO MORE TEARDROPS
TONIGHT
UNTIL YESTERDAY (NON E LA PIOGGIA)
THE BOULEVARD OF BROKEN DREAMS
JUST SAY I LOVE HER
NO ONE WILL EVER KNOW
ANYWHERE I WANDER
TAKE ME
ROSES OF YESTERDAY
THE VALENTINO TANGO
JUST ONE OF THOSE THINGS
LET'S FACE THE MUSIC AND DANCE
LULLABY OF BROADWAY
LOVE WALKED IN
THESE FOOLISH THINGS
I'M JUST A LUCCKY SO AND SO

IT HAD TO BE YOU
CA, C'EST L'AMOUR
BLUES IN THE NIGHT
TAKING A CHANCE ON LOVE

**PURELY TONY BENNETT CD -
IMPORT**
SOLITAIRE
BLUE VELVET
RAGS TO RICHES
HERE IN MY HEART
COLD COLD HEART
I'M THE KING OF BROKEN HEARTS
CONGRATULATIONS TO SOMEONE
I WON'T CRY ANYMORE
BOULEVARD OF BROKEN DREAMS
OUR LADY OF FATIMA
PLEASE MY LOVE
BECAUSE OF YOU

BIBLIOGRAPHY

TONY BENNETT - SINGS RODGERS &
HART SONGS CD:
http://www.cduniverse.com/productinfo.a
sp?pid=6853136

TONY BENNETT - GREATEST HITS OF THE '60S CD:
http://www.cduniverse.com/productinfo.asp?pid=7255322

TONY BENNETT - CLOUD 7 CD:
http://www.cduniverse.com/productinfo.asp?pid=4716183

TONY BENNETT - THE MOVIE SONG ALBUM CD:
http://www.cduniverse.com/productinfo.asp?pid=1085245

TONY BENNETT - MTV UNPLUGGED CD:
http://www.cduniverse.com/productinfo.asp?pid=7255323

TONY BENNETT SINGS HIS ALL-TIME HALL OF FAME HITS CD:
http://www.cduniverse.com/productinfo.asp?pid=1088787

TONY BENNETT - SING THE ULTIMATE AMERICAN SONGBOOK VOL. 1 CD:
http://www.cduniverse.com/productinfo.asp?pid=7496407

TONY BENNETT - IF I RULED THE WORLD: SONGS FOR THE JET SET CD: http://www.cduniverse.com/productinfo.asp?pid=1088734

TONY BENNETT - BEAT OF MY HEART CD: http://www.cduniverse.com/productinfo.asp?pid=1089324

TONY BENNETT - I WANNA BE AROUND CD: http://www.cduniverse.com/productinfo.asp?pid=1089326

MY BEST TO YOU CD: http://www.cduniverse.com/productinfo.asp?pid=1113451&style=classical

TONY BENNETT - COLLECTION: I LEFT MY HEART IN SAN FRANCISCO/ART OF EXCELLENCE/ASTORIA CD: http://www.cduniverse.com/productinfo.asp?pid=6921026

TONY BENNETT - SOMETHING CD: http://www.cduniverse.com/productinfo.asp?pid=1088403

TONY BENNETT - HAVE I TOLD YOU LATELY CD:
http://www.cduniverse.com/productinfo.asp?pid=7035368

TONY BENNETT - I LEFT MY HEART IN SAN FRANCISCO CD:
http://www.cduniverse.com/productinfo.asp?pid=8251742

TONY BENNETT - GREATEST HITS OF THE '50S CD:
http://www.cduniverse.com/productinfo.asp?pid=7255357

TONY BENNETT - LIFE IS BEAUTIFUL CD:
http://www.cduniverse.com/productinfo.asp?pid=5912688

TONY BENNETT - THIS IS JAZZ #33 CD:
http://www.cduniverse.com/productinfo.asp?pid=1088593

YOUNG TONY BENNETT CD:
http://www.cduniverse.com/productinfo.asp?pid=6793547

TONY BENNETT - GOOD LIFE CD:
http://www.cduniverse.com/productinfo.asp?pid=6812984

TONY BENNETT - BENNETT/BERLIN CD:
http://www.cduniverse.com/productinfo.asp?pid=1086471

ARTIST'S CHOICE: TONY BENNETT CD:
http://www.cduniverse.com/productinfo.asp?pid=5897010

ESSENCE OF TONY BENNETT CD:
http://www.cduniverse.com/productinfo.asp?pid=1087695

TONY BENNETT - CLASSIC COLLECTION CD:
http://www.cduniverse.com/productinfo.asp?pid=7275719

TONY BENNETT - STEPPIN' OUT CD:
http://www.cduniverse.com/productinfo.asp?pid=7612006

TONY BENNETT - JAZZ CD:
http://www.cduniverse.com/productinfo.asp?pid=7612011

TONY BENNETT - JAZZ MOODS: COOL
CD:
http://www.cduniverse.com/productinfo.a
sp?pid=6846263

PLAYLIST: THE VERY BEST OF TONY
BENNETT CD:
http://www.cduniverse.com/productinfo.a
sp?pid=7725441

TONY BENNETT - MOVIE SONG ALBUM
CD:
http://www.cduniverse.com/productinfo.a
sp?pid=7612014

TONY BENNETT - ASTORIA: PORTRAIT
OF THE ARTIST CD:
http://www.cduniverse.com/productinfo.a
sp?pid=1086737

TONY BENNETT - FOR ONCE IN MY
LIFE/I'VE GOTTA BE ME CD:
http://www.cduniverse.com/productinfo.a
sp?pid=7955697

TONY BENNETT - BLUE VELVET CD:
http://www.cduniverse.com/productinfo.a
sp?pid=3605313

TONY BENNETT - I LEFT MY HEART IN SAN FRANCISCO/PERFECTLY FRANK CD:
http://www.cduniverse.com/productinfo.asp?pid=8280785

TONY BENNETT - HAVE YOU MET MISS JONES? CD:
http://www.cduniverse.com/productinfo.asp?pid=1950087

TONY BENNETT - PERFECTLY FRANK CD:
http://www.cduniverse.com/productinfo.asp?pid=7652021

TONY BENNETT - VERY THOUGHT OF YOU CD:
http://www.cduniverse.com/productinfo.asp?pid=1113389

TONY BENNETT - WHO CAN I TURN TO CD:
http://www.cduniverse.com/productinfo.asp?pid=6804517

TONY BENNETT - COLLECTIONS CD:
http://www.cduniverse.com/productinfo.asp?pid=7447643

TONY BENNETT - PLAYIN' WITH MY FRIENDS: BENNETT SINGS THE BLUES CD:
http://www.cduniverse.com/productinfo.asp?pid=8251661

TONY BENNETT - SINGIN' AND SWINGIN' CD:
http://www.cduniverse.com/productinfo.asp?pid=2209260

TONY BENNETT - STRANGER IN PARADISE CD:
http://www.cduniverse.com/productinfo.asp?pid=7753281

TONY BENNETT - RAGS TO RICHES: 23 EARLY HITS AND FAVORITES CD:
http://www.cduniverse.com/productinfo.asp?pid=7059697

IN CONCERT CD – IMPORT:
http://www.cduniverse.com/productinfo.asp?pid=6920409&style=classical

TONY BENNETT - ART OF ROMANCE CD:
http://www.cduniverse.com/productinfo.asp?pid=7985199

TONY BENNETT - SONGS FROM THE HEART CD – IMPORT:
http://www.cduniverse.com/productinfo.asp?pid=1389124

TONY BENNETT - PLATINUM ANTHOLOGY CD:
http://www.cduniverse.com/productinfo.asp?pid=7748899

TONY BENNETT - BENNETT SINGS ELLINGTON: HOT & COOL CD:
http://www.cduniverse.com/productinfo.asp?pid=7623556

ONLY THE BEST OF TONY BENNETT CD:
http://www.cduniverse.com/productinfo.asp?pid=7938212

TONY BENNETT - YOUNG TONY CD – IMPORT:
http://www.cduniverse.com/productinfo.asp?pid=7392532

TONY BENNETT - PURELY CD – IMPORT:
http://www.cduniverse.com/productinfo.asp?pid=7920576

TONY BENNETT - BEST SINGER IN THE BUSINESS CD – IMPORT:
http://www.cduniverse.com/productinfo.asp?pid=6848943

TONY BENNETT - 16 MOST REQUESTED SONGS CD – IMPORT:
http://www.cduniverse.com/productinfo.asp?pid=2074701

TONY BENNETT - CLASSIC BENNETT: JAZZ SIDES CD – IMPORT:
http://www.cduniverse.com/productinfo.asp?pid=7903384

TONY BENNETT - CLASSIC ALBUM COLLECTION CD – IMPORT:
http://www.cduniverse.com/productinfo.asp?pid=7795548

TONY BENNETT - WHILE WE'RE YOUNG CD – IMPORT:
http://www.cduniverse.com/productinfo.asp?pid=7059075

TONY BENNETT CD – IMPORT:
http://www.cduniverse.com/productinfo.asp?pid=7447704

TONY BENNETT - CHICAGO CD – IMPORT:
http://www.cduniverse.com/productinfo.asp?pid=3112788

TONY BENNETT - LET THERE BE LOVE CD – IMPORT:
http://www.cduniverse.com/productinfo.asp?pid=7776796

TONY BENNETT - LIFE IS A SONG CD – IMPORT:
http://www.cduniverse.com/productinfo.asp?pid=7321502

TONY BENNETT - ORIGINALS CD – IMPORT:
http://www.cduniverse.com/productinfo.asp?pid=7466830

TONY BENNETT - PURELY CD – IMPORT:
http://www.cduniverse.com/productinfo.asp?pid=7653550

ABOUT THE AUTHOR

I was 59 years old; a mother of three very special and supportive adult children and a grandmother of three wonderful grandsons (I now have five grand-children.) when I started writing my first book whilst watching a Bon Jovi concert DVD. (I am an avid fan, if you can call me that; crazy is more like it.)

I write from the heart and I really enjoyed writing the book so I wrote another using a different artist, and the books kept coming to me and I kept writing them.(with a little help from above)

Because I use different artist/artists song titles I have to be very careful with Copyright so a lot of legal requirements have to be taken into consideration before publishing the books. I also needed a name that would connect my books to each other; so the "Song Title Series" books began.

All my books are short stories; however it depends on how many song titles there are to be used, as to the length of the book. Some artists didn't have enough song titles on their own so I combined them with a few other artists. Other artists had that many song titles that I could have written a novel; but it would have ended up being boring.

Challenges I like, so writing books with various artists are a lot of fun and require careful thinking.

Why should I have all the fun writing the books and not be able to share them with everyone; so I have converted them into large print books so that you can share my fun as well.

Hopefully in the not too distant future; the books will also be available as audio books so that no-one will miss out on my fun and enjoyment of writing these unique books. I hope that you enjoy reading them.

My web site www.songtitleseries.com is the place to visit for updates of new books and a place to purchase other titles in other formats.

OTHER BOOKS IN THE
SONG TITLE SERIES

Bon Jovi – Wanted Dead Or Alive
Green Day
AC/DC
Beach Boys
Slim Dusty
Country Women
Five Country Men
Six Crooners
Three Crooners
ABBA
The Rat Pack
Elton John
Classic 50s & 60s Rock 'N' Roll

TESTIMONIALS

I am Susie and would like to tell you guys, how much I am enjoying Joan Maguire's Books!! They are very enjoyable, and they are something that you do not ever want to put down!! I really enjoy these books; I can't wait until the next one that she puts out!!!!!!! I say go to your local book store, today and get one, you will not be disappointed!!!!! Sue-from the United States of America

The song titles series are books that were intriguing and were hard to believe that these short stories were written within the incorporated song titles of the artists that are mentioned in the titles. I loved what I have read so far and think that anyone with an imagination and love of music as the author you will surely enjoy reading these.
L.K. Brisbane Australia.

After reading through your range of books I felt I must compliment you Joan on the imaginative and entertaining way in which you presented each group and the Musicians in those groups. The way the stories were constructed is a credit to your work ethic. These must have taken considerable time to piece together and it is obviously a work of love for you.
I wish you all the success you truly deserve and look forward to seeing you next time you visit Tamworth.
Peter Harkins   Managing Director Cheapa Music   Country Music Capital Tamworth

Joan Maguire Books are very nice, I enjoy reading them so much, they are hard to put down!! Especially when she does one about Bonjovi and their songs!!!
If I can say, it is worth every penny, when you buy one!!! The Books make nice presents, for a person whom loves to read!!! I can guarantee that you will LOVE these books, because I do!!!!!!!!!
Dawn from Newark, Delaware in the United States of America